T0195822

Moments on the Train

ESSIE SAPP-BENSON

authorHOUSE

AuthorHouse™
1663 Liberty Drive
Bloomington, IN 47403
www.authorhouse.com
Phone: 833-262-8899

Published by AuthorHouse 06/22/2021

ISBN: 978-1-6655-2081-2 (sc)
ISBN: 978-1-6655-2082-9 (hc)
ISBN: 978-1-6655-2080-5 (e)

Library of Congress Control Number: 2021906211

Print information available on the last page.

Any people depicted in stock imagery provided by Getty Images are models, and such images are being used for illustrative purposes only. Certain stock imagery © Getty Images.

This book is printed on acid-free paper.

To G, my Guide, My Guardian. Thanks for
sustaining me throughout the years.

What's Going On

-Marvin Gaye

My name is June Calloway. During the late 90's through the beginning of the new millennium, I kept a daily journal as I traveled on the train to and from work. It became a form of meditation, a way to maintain my sanity. I was in a long-term relationship with a man who was addicted to crack-cocaine and I was working a stressful job as a county case-manager in Atlanta. I thought it couldn't get any worse. Throughout my life, I have felt the presence of a guide, a guardian who protected me and kept me in the care of the Most High. To me, she was simply 'G.'

With G's blessings. I'm here to share my journey.

4/9/96
Journal Entry

Morning, G. Rolling on Marta train. Didn't get up until 5:35 am. Aside from it's positive effects, Valium also makes me feel tired. However, I managed to pull myself together and get going. Paul moaned that it's probably inevitable that he go to jail next week. His hearing was reset for April 16.

"Did you call Mr. Adams at the bank?" I asked, placing my lunch in my over-sized bag.

"Twice, but he hasn't returned my call," he said. I can see that the pressure is getting to him. It's getting on my nerves, too.

"Call him and see if he'll accept half of the payment," I said, on my way out the door.

I called Paul at home after I got to work.

"Do you have another number for Mr. Adams, Paul?

"No," he said.

Opening my personal phone book, I gave him Mr. Adams number at the bank and hung up. Paul had been sullen this morning. He feels I'm wrong for bringing this action against him. Well, it's just too bad. And maybe this is what crazy looks like because we're supposed to be a couple---caring and sharing with each other, but I'm the one who's been inconvenienced and it looks as though I may have to pay all or most of the money back anyway. So I'm not going to worry about his feelings. He wasn't worried about mine when he took a thousand dollars from my checking account. Just wrote himself a check without my knowledge.

Checks bounced and things went crazy, right at Christmas time, too. That was so fowl! He's never done that before. He's done a lot of things, but not like that. He's addicted to Crack, you see.

When I got home, Paul was sprawled on the chair. There were two large pill-containers on the counter.

"What's all that?" I asked

"Goddam pills I got from the VA."

"For what," I asked.

"My blood pressure. When the nurse took my pressure, she got all excited and forced me into a wheelchair until I saw the doctor!"

I looked at him. He looked okay to me, maybe a little tired. Forget what he said the figures were for his pressure, but apparently it was alarming.

"Want to play a game of Scrabble, or would that shoot your pressure up?" I'm trying to lighten things up.

"Nope, want to see if the pills I took are gonna make me drowsy."

I could see that he was already drowsy. A few minutes later he was zonked out. He awoke just as the news was going off grumbling that he'd missed it. I made myself a grilled cheese sandwich, had a glass of wine and settled in to watch a PBS special 'The Shape of the World' which Paul wasn't too thrilled about. He was waiting on the NBA finals and Sports. I did the dishes and was in bed by 9:30.

4/13/96
Journal Entry

Rolling on Marta Rail
Morning, G. All blessings to the Most High

Paul was all pensive and quiet this morning. I wasn't in a good mood either. Got up late. Weekend was nothing to brag about. Clayton came over with a bottle of Rum and we sat around for a while. Mostly we talked about Paul. He was as disappointed and confused as I was concerning Paul. He wanted to talk to him, they're like brothers. But he said to me, "Save yourself, you can't save him. I don't like what he's doing to you." He swiped at his eyes and I looked away.

Paul didn't show up until after 9:00 o'clock. He and some brother named Don came in together. Looking sideways at Clayton and away from me, he explained that one of the tires went out and there was no spare, so he had to leave the car on Campbellton Road, near Oakland City Train Station. I was furious but managed to keep hold of myself for the moment. Clayton prepared to leave, looking disgusted. He knew what the deal was. Paul and this brother, Don, had been out smoking. And yet Clayton offered to drop Don off at the train station. That's just Clayton, considerate and caring. Don nearly tripped over his own feet trying to get out of there. I went to bed angry.

Saturday, I confronted Paul about the car. He had the nerve to tell me he could do nothing about the fact that it was just sitting where he'd left it (I prayed it was still there)! We had no cash on hand to speak of.

He finally concluded that he was going to have to hook up with one of his street people to get the car home and see about getting it fixed when he gets his VA Disability check.

After he left, my friend and neighbor, Barb, came over for coffee and she washed and conditioned my hair. When Paul returned (he got the car home some-how), Barb cut his hair and gave him a decent line. She's good and she's convenient and inexpensive. After I did some cleaning, Paul and I played several sets of Scrabble. Yeah, I calmed down, since he, at least, got the car home, G. After that I stretched out on the bed and browsed through my New Yorker before dozing.

6/1/96
Journal Entry

Out here rolling on Marta

Been awhile, huh, G? Guess I'm just lazy. My stomach's acting up, got a prescription for Tagamet and it's finally kicking in. Not much to talk about. Paul and I are going through again. We had it out on Saturday when he came home after a three-day binge. At first I didn't let him in. I could see him approaching from the window. He knocked and knocked and I refused to let him in. Man I was angry! For a moment I thought he was gone until he startled me by knocking on the patio window as I passed it on my way to the kitchen. Fearing he'd start kicking the patio door or something, I let him in. He did most of the talking. I'd heard it all before. About how he was going to stop smoking crack. At one point he grabbed my hands, forcing me to look at him. I snatched away, didn't want him to touch me, so sick of his lies.

"I'm going to tell my therapist everything, June," he said. "I'm not going to hold back anything this time. But I won't get to see her for another two weeks. If I can just clear my system out and stay clean until then, you know? Yeah, that would be good, wouldn't it?"

I didn't answer him. I know if he does stay clean and make it in to see her, he's not going to tell her everything, like how the cocaine eases his back pain better than any of the pain meds he's taking. How it almost makes him feel normal for days and when he comes down, he's back into that cycle of chronic pain that never goes away. He won't tell her that because he's afraid she just may conclude that he's making excuses for himself. We've had this conversation many times. This is his thinking, G, not mine. I believe he's paranoid.

11/26/96
Journal Entry

At Garnett Station, headed to the IBEW office. Long time, right, G? What can I say? I know you know. Just been busy living life, doing the best I can, trying to make it.

Had a weird experience earlier today. I was sitting at my desk preparing appointment letters to mail out, when suddenly my vision blurred. The white paper in front of me seemed to burn my eyes. I quickly pushed my chair back from the desk and tried to focus. I felt severe pain on the left side of my head. I sat there for a few minutes, then pulled myself forward and continued with my letters. A few minutes later I stopped, my vision blurred even more still. I couldn't work like this. I put my hands over my face to shield my eyes from the glare. My head was pounding! When my vision finally cleared a little, I got up and made my way down the hall and into the elevator and down to the first floor to the eye-doctor's office. Thank goodness we work in a Union Building, we have some of everything in here. Anyway, I explained what had happened to the doctor. She asked if I had high-blood pressure. I shook my head, no.

"Well, if you have problems with your monthly cycle, it's not uncommon to suffer with migraine headaches. The blurred vision you described and the pain on one side of your head indicates the beginning of a migraine headache," she said. She peered at me closely while she spoke.

I groaned inside. God knows I suffer severe cramps during my cycle, is this now going to be an additional headache (pun intended) every month?!

"If the pain gets any worse and especially if your vision becomes blurred again, I want you back in my office this afternoon. I'll take a look behind your eyes to make sure there's nothing behind them."

"Thanks," I said. I have no intentions of returning to her office. I'm just stressed the hell-out, that's all!

3/29/97
Journal Entry

B een a minute, huh, G? You know what it's been.
Stacy had to turn in 39 cases today, she was frantic all day! John claimed he had a virus and wanted to be left alone. Victor's fiancé is in town and they met for lunch and he never returned to the office. Cora was upset because of where her computer was placed. Everyone was in a fowl mood including me. While eating in the cafeteria, Elaine came and sat across from me uninvited and began running her mouth non-stop about nothing, absolutely nothing. Honestly, I didn't want to be bothered, just wanted to relax and gather my thoughts. Every few seconds she stopped to cough. She absolutely didn't even bother to cover her mouth---sitting directly across from me and my burger!

"Will you please cover your mouth, Elaine?" I said loudly.

She looked wounded and her silly face turned candy-cotton pink (she's a white sister) as she bolted from the table. Good riddens! I didn't care. I mean, I just don't understand people like that! Sitting there coughing all over my food, yuck!

5/4/97
Journal Entry

8:35 p.m.

I'm shaken, G. Two plain-clothes detectives came into the back door with Paul. They said that they'd received complaints that he was dealing drugs in the neighborhood and they wanted to see some identification. The one who spoke followed Paul upstairs when he went to get his ID. After a few minutes, I started up the stairs, feeling uneasy. The second detective stopped me.

"It would be safer for both of us if you don't follow Mr. Calloway upstairs," he said.

I was so upset, for a moment I thought, "Mr. Calloway! Then I realized he meant Paul. And suddenly I'm 'Really' concerned for Pauls' safety. You know what I'm saying, G?

"But I want to be with him," I said, knowing it was futile.

"It would be safer for both of us if you don't follow Mr. Calloway upstairs," he said again.

He had a thick crop of reddish-brown hair and smelled minty--- probably gum that he kept snapping as his eyes shifted around the room. He was really taking it all in. Irritating son of a bitch! Oops, sorry, G.

I came back down the stairs and sat on the couch. Out of nowhere a third plain-clothes officer stepped into the living room from the dining area. Stunned, I asked him if he was a cop, too (very foolish question). He nodded that he was. Shortly afterwards, Paul and the speaking cop came downstairs. He then warned Paul in a threatening manner that they were watching him and that he'd better be careful because of the tip they'd gotten about him. Paul said that he wasn't doing anything wrong. The officer ignored him and repeated his warning (what are these guys, robots or something?). Then, Paul followed the three of them out onto the back patio which is where they'd entered. I peered out the dining-room window when Paul didn't immediately come back in. People were driving in and out of the all-night Food-Mart next door where Paul was supposedly seen selling drugs. It was very busy as usual, folks pumping gas, purchasing beer, wine, and cigarettes. A man threw a glass of something out of a plastic cup as he turned on his windshield wipers. I stared, trying to see something, not knowing exactly what. A young guy swaggered past with an umbrella swinging in his hand. Why didn't he open it up, it was raining, though not hard. A Day and Night cab raced past, cutting a sharp turn at the corner, splashing muddy water in mid-air. Two teenagers stood in the center of the parking-lot with brown paper bags in their hands. A young heavy-hipped sister in skin-tight jeans and white-framed glasses stood near the store entrance. I recognized the little fat boy who was caught stealing a couple of days ago, he stood at attention at the side of the building staring at Ali, the store owner, apparently being further chastised. An elderly, conservative-dressed brother screeched to a halt... Further down the building, on the same side, a young, high-yellow brother stood in the shadows, barely visible. I couldn't really see his face, as it was dusk dark out by now, but I saw his head going back and forth as if watching everything and maybe looking for something or someone. He was wearing a light-colored rain-coat or trench-coat, I couldn't tell which, but he stepped deeper into the shadows and faced the wall each time a car entered the lot and the lights faced him, hands in his pockets. Up to something for sure. No surprise here. Look, I'm from the hood. G, you know that. You learn early to know only enough to keep yourself safe and the rest...well, you mind your own business. Half the people who were up to no good were people you'd known all your life, friends and family even. Most had to hustle to make it.

As far as the Food Mart is concerned, I believe Ali may have dropped a dime on Paul. I know Paul isn't dealing drugs over there. He's too caught up in using, but he's become a nuisance to Ali because he's always there, steering customers to the dealers, hooking them up, you know. And also, last year, I reported Ali to the USDA for accepting Food Stamps for non-food items and selling alcoholic beverages and drug paraphernalia to teens. Paul was pissed, I didn't tell him until after the fact, but I couldn't help it, after all, I work and care for my people and Ali is making millions of dollars right on this corner next to all of my people who are struggling. Fuck Ali. He was fined or something and I just think he knows that I had something to do with it.

From the patio window, Paul and the speaking cop appeared to be in deep conversation, both were leaning against the railing casually speaking in hushed tones. The other two men were nowhere in sight. Odd, I thought.

5/20/97
Journal entry

It's humid as all get-out this morning. I'm running late. It's cloudy and rain's expected any moment.

The female bus driver is laughing with one of the passengers. Campbellton Road is being worked on for a long stretch. They're widening it---it's a main drag.

A female in the back is chatting robustly, non-stop about a bad relationship. We've finally reached the station, barely made the train.

Lunch-delicious turkey sandwich from the cafeteria. The office is freezing but I'm not complaining. I had Slim, the maintenance guy, open the vent over my desk yesterday.

My stomach's slightly upset since this morning. Due to that glass of milk last night, I guess. I'm sitting in the cafeteria having coffee and a cigarette while writing. I don't remember this guy's name coming toward me. He's an Employment Services Supervisor who trained us on a new program on the System several weeks ago. We talked about the poor ventilation in the building for a minute.

"Never been in a DFACS building that's properly ventilated," he says. He squashes his cigarette out in the tiny ashtray, stands abruptly, turns and walks away.

I called home earlier and spoke with Paul.
"Were you asleep?"
"No," he said.
"How're you feeling?"

"Not too good," he said.

Silence.

"I'll talk with you later, you sound groggy, okay?"

"Okay."

Paula just waved at me from across the room, she's smoking a cigarette.

At 2:15, I left work for a 3:00 appointment with Dr. Meadows for a follow-up visit. Travelling west, mostly young black men on the train. Several teen mothers with their young babies. A young mother sits across from me with child in her arms. She looks as if she has a lot on her mind, head cast down, child sucking on thumb. Big, sad eyes. Two young black brothers in business attire conversing quietly.

Directly, behind me, someone is bragging about shooting someone.

"And Montel trying to act like he still got some animosity. You know I had to shoot him in the arm! Shot him on the side of the building while he was taking a piss! Yeah, man, had to do it!"

I refrained from shaking my head.

Got off at Hightower Station and caught the 165. This is usually a long wait—maybe fifteen minutes. I have no idea how long the driver's been sitting.

Well, back at the Doctor's office. This is hopefully my last visit. He removed the last stitch out of the back of my neck where he'd removed a tiny growth last week. He says I'm going to be fine. The cyst was benign, thankfully.

Sitting at Five-Points, waiting on the 82 to go home. It's cooling off. There's a nice breeze but it's sure to rain soon. People passing by staring directly into my eyes and then examining me from head to toe. I catch myself looking down, thinking maybe my top is open or something. What's up with that?

On my way home. Love this ride, very scenic. We'll travel up through the Cascade area where there are many nice homes, old and new. This is an all-black area, there's a golf course, parks and woods. It includes Benjamin E. Mays Dr., Cascade Rd., Lynway Dr, Harlin and Landrum Rds. Then there's Childress, Mt. Gilead, Meadows

Lane Dr., Dale Lane (there's a beautiful home for sale on this street). Finally, we're up near Greenbriar Mall. Several more stops and I'll be home. Past Headland Dr, Sun Trust Bank (a black bank), then, thankfully, my stop.

5/21/97
Journal Entry

Father, thank you for this new day. I look forward to each moment. I know that I'm whole, healthy and that I have everything I need. Morning, G.

Last night I read into the wee hours. I'm nearly finished with "Laying in the Bed You Made" by Virginia De'Berry and Donna Grant. Pretty good read.

It's a beautiful morning. Boo Coo people boarding this train. Most of the seated passengers are asleep or resting with their eyes closed. Some are staring at nothing. I'm already sleepy myself. Haven't had any coffee yet.

Evening:

Got off at Five Points Station and stopped in the new downtown Kroger a little while ago. Wanted to see what it's like. Just opened recently to accommodate the new crowd moving into the new Condos and High-rises down here. The store is huge inside with long isles and a large, colorful variety of prepared meals; salads, sushi, pasta, sandwiches, etc. Over-priced, of course. Nice lay-out, though. If I worked in our downtown office, I'd check it out for sure.

Before I left the office this evening, I called Paul.

"Social Security denied me on the phone," he said.

"Well, we knew this could happen, Paul. You haven't gotten written notification yet though, right?"

"No, they didn't even have my correct address," he said.

"Make them give it to you in writing, Paul, they can't just tell you you're ineligible if you submit a formal application. But really, you've got to throw your hat back in to VA." I hated bringing this up, they've denied him twice even though he was injured in the service and it's well-documented, but it's his crack-addiction that they have a problem with. We both feel he's getting the business because of this.

"I just don't care. Fuck it," he said.

"Yes you do, Paul. Stay with it, babe."

5/22/97
Journal Entry

L ord, I'm exhausted. Today was a good day, however. Got plenty of work done. I'm off tomorrow and Monday's Memorial Day. The Book Club meets this Saturday. I plan to do some writing and personal organizing this weekend. Exercise and meditate on Sunday, even if just for an hour or so. This is very important to me now. It helps.

5/24/97
Journal Entry

On Northbound train headed to Nita's for the Book Club Meeting. It wasn't easy getting out of the house. I'm always lounging around on Saturdays. It's good to be out and about, however, hope everyone shows up. Got my tape-recorder. It's threatening rain. Shouldn't be too late. I don't want to be the first one there. Don't want to be last, either. Wish I'd put in some time meditating this morning. I will tomorrow as planned. Did manage to exercise and do the daily word thing. Paul made salmon this morning which was delicious, as usual. I'm proud of my progress exercising. I'm doing between four hundred to five hundred crunches most mornings.

We're at Five Points right now. It's very humid. Trains are running slow. That's the way it is on weekends, no rush hours. Jesus, how long have I been doing this! It never gets any easier. I was fortunate to get transferred to the Northwest Office which is located directly in front of the Hightower Train Station which means you don't have to drive and most of the staff... well, about half of them, choose to ride Marta and save wear and tear on their car. I chose to save for a new car at this time. I junked my old ride after Paul left it on the street some time back. It would have cost a fortune to repair. Rent's so high, can't really afford a car payment right now anyway. Paul's only income is a small pension he gets from the bank he used to work for years ago and a partial VA Disability Check.

Beginning to cool off, thank goodness. Train finally arrived. It's about 2:00 o'clock. There's white folk on the train with their small children. You can tell that most of them only ride the trains on weekends. They're sight-seeing, pointing out important sites while on their way to the zoo, a circus, or The King Center. The kids are excited and full of chatter. Some folks stare, while others try to avoid eye contact. Now we're at the Arts Center, I think the Medical Center is next. I asked a passenger if I should get off at the next station which turned out to be Lindberg.

"Yes, get off there and get the Dunwoody train. It'll stop at the Medical Center."

Of course I should have left home earlier. What else is new!

Dunwoody is the North-bound train. Doraville is the North-east train. I have to remember this. There's now a Buckhead Station. It's fairly new. Not long ago there was a lot of hoopla about it. Folks were saying ritzy Buckhead wanted the inner-city (translation-black and Latino) people to come out and clean their homes but didn't want them having easy access and coming out to party in the clubs and restaurants, blah, blah, blah, you know, G? Me, I can't figure how anyone would take an apartment this far out and drive into Atlanta to work, daily. I mean, it's nice and all, but I wouldn't even buy anything this far out. But that's just me. Will I change my tune when the time comes?

"What time does the number 85 come," I ask a female commuter.

"At 2:39," she says.

"What time do you have now, please?"

"It's 2:20."

Okay, so that's not very long. Man, I hate being a slave to time.

It's finally here. Looks as if he's going to pull off any minute. I'm on it and he did.

A heavy white sister sits down next to me.

"Oh, I have a book just like yours," she says

"The cover is the same, there's blank pages on the inside."

"So is mine," I say. I busy myself writing with my head down, trying to convey that I'm not interested in a conversation. Someone gets off and my companion immediately gets up and takes the empty seat. For this I'm grateful because she pretty much had me squeezed in.

There's a couple sitting in lounge chairs, both blond, on the corner here at Glendale Parkway. They're dressed in evening attire—he in a black tux and she in a black-sequined dress and heels. They're sipping on something and laughing loudly. Going somewhere interesting, I suppose.

Headed home. Meeting was good. We had a wild conversation, everyone talking at one-time! Nita made Daiquiri cocktails, I brought wine, others brought hot wings, chips, dip, celery and carrots, etc. Nita had smooth jazz playing at a low volume. Everyone said they enjoyed the book. It was nice, everyone seemed to feel at home.

I'm lucky this evening. The southbound train came as soon as I reached the station and the bus was waiting at Oakland City Station when I got here. The bus is crowded, noisy and musty, mixed with the smell of Popeye's Chicken, Crispy Crème Donuts, barbecued ribs, alcohol and sweat. Now I'm nauseous! Geez. I should have called Paul to meet me but it's too late now. I pull a small bottle of water from my book bag and take small sips slowly.

Campbellton Road is wide open as usual, especially on a Saturday evening. Liquor stores, fast food joints, gas stations, corner stores and street corners are all crowded. Some of these stops are pitch-black, however. It's amazing, you'd think you're on a country road on these particular stops.

A couple just sat down, obviously feeling no pain as they stumbled to find seats. Must have just left Marco's, the jazz club across the street. It appears to be packed already. Real popular for their 'Happy Hour' with the live jazz band. I haven't been there in a minute. It used to be my spot when I first hit the Atlanta scene. Cars are everywhere. The bus is vibrating from the music.

6/2/97
Journal Entry

Waiting on the #82

Betty Shabazz was severely burned last night! A neighbor put a sheet over her. Eighty percent of her body has 3rd degree burns. She's clinging to life. They suspect her 12 year old grandson! He was found wandering the streets in a daze and smelling of flamant, according to the news. This is the son whose mother was in the news a couple of years ago for attempting to kill Louis Farrakhan while dating a white brother. These events prompted Ms. Shabazz to publicly acknowledge that Mr. Farrakhan is not her enemy. She had long accused him of being involved in her husbands' assassination. What a sad day this is! What a tragedy!

This past weekend, Paul went out, after meeting me at Oakland City Station and giving me a hundred dollars. I didn't see him again until Sunday morning. He was ill and complained that his left arm was numb. He stayed on the couch all day and said he didn't feel up to taking a shower. I regarded him solemnly and placed his socks and shoes on the patio. Neither of us slept much last night. I give thanks each time he makes it home safely. I do love him. You know that, G. But it's difficult... when he walks in sick, disoriented, paranoid and depressed... I keep praying that the Creator will take this desire from him and that, somehow, I may be shown the best way to help him without hurting myself. And I keep praying that I can reach the joy that I know resides in me, G. I have no answers. I lay awake amazed that someone can continue putting themselves through this. He seems to care nothing for himself, yet I know that appearances are deceptive. He's an addict, pure and simple. I keep praying that this awful binging cycle will end. At the same time, there is much to give thanks for. We've both grown somewhat in relating to each other, but just as soon as things begin improving, the cycle begins all over. At these times, I ask myself if I care anything about myself. What's my excuse, G?

Later: On evening train:

Productive day even though I didn't feel well. Sinus issues, not enough sleep, etc. These school kids are loud as all get out on this train.

Kim, from Georgia State University, called me on Sunday regarding the part-time position in the Social Work Dept. All I know is that it entails phone surveys requesting answers on social/political issues. Hopefully, it won't be too tedious or boring. I plan to work 12 hours a week minimum. Really can use the money.

My friend, Brenda, also called. Says she and Frank are back together and that they're getting remarried! Unbelievable! These two just got divorced last year! My circle, gotta love'em! What can I say? There's no accounting for why you love and care about certain people. For me, I've always loved folks who are fearless about being who they are, regardless of how others see them. I always find them most interesting. Irritating and sometimes frustrating, but authentic, truthful... they're like fresh-air, I can breathe and be myself around them. I detest artificial people, they depress me.

6/3/97
Journal Entry

Timothy McVey was found guilty of all charges yesterday. The sentencing phase is today. Witnesses said he showed no emotions at the verdict.

This morning, Paul made noises about not feeling like going to VA.

"I'm going to tell the doctor that I need to be hospitalized," he said. "My stomach is messing with me, I'm losing weight and I'm too depressed to do anything, man. Probably won't do any good though," he said. His doctor is a young no-nonsense guy, shoots straight about Paul's health, not sympathetic at all, unlike his previous doctor who was much older and more familiar with disabled vets and their needs. I wish they would hospitalize him. He's afraid to get the blood exam that they said he should get. It's been scheduled for some time in July. He failed to show for the original appointment and he has lost a lot of weight. I just don't know. God be with him. Us.

6/4/97
Journal Entry

Father, please let me get some sleep tonight. I'm so weary. I haven't seen Paul since yesterday morning.

6/5/97
Journal Entry

P aul came in about 3:30 am this morning. I didn't get up or say anything to him. Neither of us spoke when I got up, showered and dressed. I called home mid-morning.

"Please don't put anything on the stove and lay on the couch, Paul," I said. "You may fall asleep."

"Oh, I'm fine," he said, using what I called his professional voice, which really pissed me off. When he does that (which he does frequently when he comes off of a binge) it reminds me of one of my mom's frequent quotes; "A man can lie in the gutter and do all kinds of low-down things in the streets and then come home, get up the next morning and put on a shirt and tie and still be called Mr. Johnson. But a woman can't do that. Your reputation is all you've got, hold on to it. Always remember that." I know she spoke from experience, she'd been through it all with my dad. According to her, he'd come from an educated black family in Georgia, teachers and preachers, proud people. But he was the 'black sheep' among his siblings, the baby…never accomplishing much. She never had much good to say about him. She once told me that aside from my looks, the only thing I got from my dad was the idea that I was something special, and that that wasn't good. She said that I held my head too high and threw away things too soon and that I had Champaign taste but didn't have a pot to piss in or a window to throw it out of, just like my dad. That hurt. But being a single teen-mom, guess I believed her. I had no one to tell me different. My father had left her when I was just a toddler and the only father-figure I had was my uncle, mom's brother, a lovable alcoholic (whom I dearly loved) that she eventually had to take care of.

"Where've you been for two days, Paul?"

"My usual place. Hey, listen, let's not do this now, I'm trying to hear something right now."

As if he was the dutiful partner and I'd interrupted something important and beneficial to us both, he's good at that. I slammed the phone down hard in his ear, furious! I knew he was watching C-SPAN. What's the point? I still didn't know if he'd actually kept his VA appointment. And what is this reluctance to go to NA meetings regularly, get a sponsor and all that? Yeah, he dibbles and dabbles, goes to meetings here and there, but not nearly like he should! Church...we both go irregularly. I don't know... we need help, G! What is it with you? You ride with me daily, you're at my side in our home, when I lay down at night, you're ever-present... why in the hell won't you intervene, you know our whole story, our needs, what the fuck... are you my spiritual guide or not?!

Later:

G... I'm sorry, I had no right... I mean, I get so frustrated! Please don't give up on me, you're my pipeline, my access to the Most High. The world is an awful and fearful place without you by my side. Forgive me...please.

Got off at Five Points and walked to the Main Library on Peachtree. They're having a 'Friends of the Library' book sale. Found some great stuff; a couple of classics, a few 'short story' collections and one biography. I browsed a couple of hours and got eight books for twenty-three dollars. Not bad! Love these sales.

6/6/97
Journal entry

O n my way to this part-time gig. Going to be late, can't seem to escape this tardiness thing lately. Oh, well, no need to dwell on it, my main focus right now, is to get in there and learn the job today. I feel hyped, not sure why. Maybe it's the cigarettes and exercising and all that coffee. Got to give up the cigarettes. Truly.

Later:

Got off the train at the West End Station just to browse. This area always fascinates me. It's a historic area. There's a mixture of ethnic and spiritual groups crowding the sidewalks and restaurants twenty-four-seven. Jamil Al-Amin, formerly known as Rap Brown lives in this area. Muslims, so-called Black Israelites, Africans, Jamaicans, Rastafarians, mostly all black and all thriving peacefully together. Muslims on the corner selling Mohammad Speaks newspapers and Bean Pies. Israelite Vegetarian Restaurants, African restaurants. Of course, there's your regular African American drug dealers, hustlers and thieves. (Word on the street is that Jamil Al-Amin and his people have run many of the drug dealers out, cleaned up a lot of crime and so forth). Lots of Black Art dealers selling their wares on the street. If you're looking for afro-centric clothing, you can find some great looking stuff at the West End Mall. All part of the neighborhood. There's delicious Crispy Crème donuts. You can smell them and the coffee, Popeye's and Churches Chicken and McDonalds all mingled in together. The streets are lined with old historical homes which have been restored and sold at astronomical cost. Gentrification, they call it. Enter the white folks. They're buying up these homes like crazy, happy for the short commute to their downtown offices!

6/7/97
Journal Entry

Sitting here, writing, waiting on the #82 bus. A tan-colored van comes screeching to the curb, a female driver. Immediately, I'm on guard. It's a beautiful Saturday afternoon, but it doesn't matter, you can't be too careful around here. I place my hand inside my purse and leave it there as she jumps quickly from the van, in my face before I know it, invading my space, too close for comfort. I move my hand inside my purse as if to withdraw it. I could have had a gun for all she knew. She withdrew, slightly and smiled but her hands were trembling.

"Excuse me, do you need a Marta Card?" she said quickly.

"A weekly card?" I ask, hesitantly.

"Well, yes, it's only good through tomorrow, but I won't be needing it this weekend, no need for it to go to waste." She was dark and heavy with a thin mustache line. Then I see a young boy on the passenger side of the van. He had her smile. I relaxed a little and extended my hand.

"Ah, thank you very much, I really appreciate this."

"Is it so strange for me to give you this?" She's still smiling...too brightly, for me.

"Well-yeah, people don't just appear and give you something...! Why did I say this? I sure didn't want a long drawn-out explanation. But she acknowledged me with a cheerful nod and jumped into her van and drove off. It was a small, good thing, someone I didn't know giving me something merely out of good will. It's sad that I felt apprehensive. But today, a stranger stopping you on the streets of Atlanta, you don't know what to expect. Just the way it is. Two females, one black and one white, just robbed a bank last week. Females!

I didn't get a chance to comment after my first day on this part-time gig yesterday, G. Anyway, it's boring! Repeatedly making calls and getting no response. Most of the calls I made were either unanswered, busy or an answering machine. The job itself is very simple. There's a script already input into the system. You read it (without sounding as if you're reading) if you're lucky enough to get a live person at the other end. The script contains questions regarding teenagers in the household. The survey has to do with their attitude toward education and their future. The few times I was able to talk with someone, they had no teenagers in the home. It's not bad. It's temporary, I can do it for a while... I hope. Right now, I'm on my way to do four hours.

When I got home yesterday, Paul wasn't there. However, he'd gone to Kroger and bought some food. Ground beef, chicken, fish, hot dogs, coffee, salad dressing and a few other things. Apparently, he wasn't able to resist hitting the streets since he had a few coins in his pocket. I could picture him throwing the food in the lower part of the refrigerator... in his haste, he'd thrown the coffee and paper plates in there with the food. The 'pipe' was calling him. At least he'd tried. Tomorrow I'll get veggies, juice and dairy stuff. Listen to me, sound as if this is normal, don't I? And he hasn't come in yet. Well, God looks out for him, right, G? I say this all the time. I have to believe it.

The people here at Georgia State are pleasant and conversation flows easily. There's not a lot of pressure, thank goodness, enough of that on my real gig, thank you very much. Yesterday didn't start off very well, however. To begin with, Dwayne, or whatever his name is, sent me to the Department of Education building at One Park Place to complete paper work for tax purposes. Mistakenly, I went to the Employment Division. The receptionist was an idiot who apparently gets off on confusing people. I'm sure she knew where I was supposed to go after I explained my situation. Instead, she wasted my time by having me complete an application for state employment. Two of them! In retrospect, I can only blame myself, it didn't feel right in the beginning. Anyway, I got it all done eventually.

Well, made four hours. It wasn't bad at all.

On the way home. Five Points Station. It's 'all the way live' downtown here on Saturdays. Here's some brothers in all black uniforms with their heads wrapped. Not Muslims, some unknown group. Looks like the group that call themselves the Black Israelites tribe. One of them speaking:

"Yeah, God sent Aids. He sent it to destroy you black brothers who are gay and filth-ridden with disease. The faggot on IV whines 'God would not forsake me!' You are a fool, brother! God, himself, will destroy you. The white man will not tell you that you're wrong. He will offer you K-Y jellies and Latex condoms. You want the white man to give you forty acres and a mule. Some of you will settle for a job or five more cents an hour. When the white man gives you this you will forget that he held you in slavery. We want to see America destroyed. We want it totally destroyed! Then we can stand up and re-build our own communities. We want the white man to be enslaved!" This brother was talking some heavy shit! Extreme, scary, just like the white-extremist groups! Too many voices out here, so much madness!

I'm exhausted and I need to eat but I'm getting off at Headland to get an Atlanta Journal, some beer and soda.

It's amazing that in four hours, I didn't complete one survey. If they were paying me based on production, I wouldn't earn a dime.

A sister in the rear of the bus is cracking her gum hard and loud. I'd like to go back there and slap her silly face! Anyone over six years old has to know that this is annoying as fuck! Downright excruciating! I'm convinced females do this to purposely annoy folks. If I was to turn around right now and catch her eye, she will give me the 'fuck you-eye roll!" Well, not today, not from me. I'm tired and irritable, just need to lean back and breathe.

6/8/97
Journal Entry

I've been up all night, G. Insomnia kicked in again. Wrote Paul a letter in the wee hours. At least I stretched out and relaxed a little. I'm fine at the moment, got to do some filing and observe Intake reviews before leaving the office. My letter to Paul was positive and to the point, hope he receives it that way.

Later:

> On the train headed home. Two older women sit across from me.
> "The world's coming to an end, honey," said one.
> "Been thinking the same thing, girl," the other one said. "The things that's happening, Ump ump, ump. It's something else out here. Even young people sayin' it!"
> The smell of the Croissant sandwich from Burger King in my bag beckons me, can't wait to get home!

> "Do you want to go to VA Hospital?" I asked Paul last night.
> "No,"
> "Would you like to go Tuesday?" I asked gently.
> "No, I'll go when I'm ready!" he bellowed. "You don't tell me when to go to the hospital. I'm trying to see how I'll feel," he sounded hoarse and weak. "And why do you always have to wake me up, huh? You always do this!" He turned over and faced the wall with a heavy sigh.
> "I knew you weren't asleep I said to the back of his head. "I heard you clicking the remote."

Waiting on train at Garnett Station. Man, around three o'clock this afternoon, I could barely keep my eyes open. I managed to straighten up the office and did file some cases. I'm prepared for Intake interviews tomorrow.

Paul was subdued when I called home earlier.

"Do you want me to pick up bread or anything," I asked.

"Doesn't matter," he muttered. I didn't ask if he'd read my letter, assuming he had.

6/10/97
Journal Entry

The gang took me to Steak & Ale for my birthday today. We had a blast! Good food. I had a steak, but the best part was the special pie they gave me because they were out of cake. It was a chocolate and vanilla deal with a wonderfully light crust. And even better was the camaraderie. We laughed and gossiped mercilessly, and I think I had three glasses of wine. I needed that, G. We didn't get back to the office until after three-thirty. Mandy pretended not to notice, she's a doll, she could have made us take a couple hours annual leave, we'd left the office at eleven-thirty! But she didn't.

6/12/97
Journal Entry

Yesterday, when I got home, Paul wasn't there. I was too tired to care and had no desire to do anything, but I pulled myself together and did two hundred-fifty crunches and then got busy. First, I cleaned the kitchen thoroughly, then I started a pot of Lima beans, seasoned with small chunks of honey-baked ham, made small cakes of corn-bread and sat down with a piece of toasted Italian bread while the beans cooked.

At nine o'clock a great movie came on. It dealt with a young woman who'd suffered brain damage after a near fatal accident. Curiously, she became addicted to sex. Her explanation was that her body would become over-heated and she would feel an over-whelming urge to have sex. And have sex she did! With anyone and everyone! As a result her family was torn apart. In the end, however, she got some help by joining a group (which was all men) with similar problems. Initially, she was aghast that these men were pedophiles, rapist and criminals! But the therapist eventually helped her to understand that all of them were suffering from an inability to control their urges and also had a lack of concern for the consequences. It was quite interesting. I watched the entire movie while pigging out on what turned out to be bean soup! Delicious. Went to bed at eleven-thirty.

Well, my day is over. Interviewed all morning and then had a short informal conference with Mandy regarding the burn-out factor of case workers. She's been with Fulton County since 1974 with only a one-year break and she's now looking forward to retirement in four years. I like

Mandy, she's easy to talk too. Apparently, she's fond of me too, or at least she likes sharing with me. This wasn't really a conference, but she closed her door to give others that impression. She has compassion for our clients as well as staff. Rare, very rare these days.

6/13/97
Journal Entry

This morning started out all wrong. Paul woke me up at five-thirty am. I'd barely slept three hours. I was irritable and tired. He wasn't in a good mood either. I had foolishly promised him I'd loan him some money. He wasn't satisfied with the amount and we argued all the way to Kroger (which is only a block down the street). Walking down the street raving like two fools, like two addicts really, anyone observing us would easily think that, G. I'm ashamed of the way I behaved and the things I said, it doesn't matter who's at fault. I hate myself when I get that way. Please God, forgive me. We both said some awful things to each other. He's an addict, what's my excuse? I'm an enabler, plain and simple. Please help us to stop the madness, G!

6/14/97
Journal Entry

Haven't heard from Paul, but in spite of that, I got a good nights' sleep. Managed to pray that mean spirit away, went shopping, treated myself by buying a couple of nice pieces at Macy's. One was a beautiful yellow skirt which flared at the bottom. Unfortunately, I can barely get it over my hips! Isn't it amazing how we women kid ourselves about our size? I should have taken the time to try it on, actually, I should have known I couldn't wear it just by looking at it! Guess I'm not accustomed to being this size, larger than I've ever been, even though I'm not heavy, but I need to be realistic about it.

After that, I went grocery shopping. Spent more time there then I needed trying to stay within my budget of a hundred dollars. I spent ninety-eight dollars and thirty-eight cents. Then I paid Mr. Ed, one of the guys who hang out in Kroger's parking lot and offer taxi services, five dollars to get me home. It was around seven when I got home. After putting away food, I phoned my sister, showered and washed my hair. By the time I fried Catfish, made a salad and sat down in front of the TV, it was after eleven. Braiding my hair was out of the question. Didn't get out of bed until after ten this morning. Had fish and two cups of coffee. Too lazy to make breakfast.

Pastor Wyley was on TV in the background. I turned it up. His message was about what he called 'enslaved minds.' He compared people's mentality with the mentality of people in times of Moses--- whose minds were enslaved by the Pharaoh. How people put their faith in jobs and material success and worry about their future continuously.

He lamented how God will bring the world under New Management and that this was Moses and Jesus's message from the beginning. He said when you submit yourself to the faith, you realize that God manages your present and future and will look out for you even when the job lays you off. It was a strong message. He said most people don't dare question authority on their jobs out of fear. He doesn't understand this and wonders why they're so anxious to question the authority in the church. There was laughter in the church at this. I got the feeling he was talking to one or two specific people in the congregation, ha ha ha.

Later:

Worked four hours at my new gig. Completed my first interview with a white teenaged male. He was obviously bored after a few minutes. Can't say I blame him. It took about twenty-five minutes. Sure helped the time pass. Uh oh… we're at Oakland City Station now and it's Saturday, hope the wait for the #83 bus isn't too long, they're really slow on weekends.

I gave Kim, the supervisor at Georgia State a copy of my ad for copy-editing. She says she'll have to clear it with her boss before I can put it on the bulletin board. Yeah, I'm hustling, trying to make that extra bread. I'm paid the same week as my regular job, wish it were other-wise. Well, I'm glad right now because there's a check waiting for me at Georgia State right now, got to pick it up.

There's some teenagers cracking on each other in front of me. Swearing and acting up. At first, I'm irritated, but then I remember I was a kid once. The boys use to do this all the time and I'm that girl who couldn't stop laughing. As long as they're not directly disrespecting the grown-ups (which they sometimes do) what can you say? Of course, the cursing is uncalled for. One of them just turned and looked directly into my face, looking embarrassed but trying to play it off.

6/15/97
Journal Entry

Didn't wake up until 9:00 am. Father, please pass this cup from me. Please send Paul home safely. In Jesus name. Amen. This fear and emotional pain is dreadful, G.

Did my hair last night, can't seem to get it the way I'd like. I'm just trippin.'

Expecting rain again today, I love it.

This bus driver is driving like a fool, he must be tired. I spent ten dollars for transportation this morning, had to get a taxi. I think I'll get a couple of hits off of this joint that my girl, Brenda, gave me. That with a can of beer, just to relax. Two of my friends frequently give me weed. They smoke on a regular basis and think I should too. Most times I accept it and stash it away for times like this. Paul has no idea. One thing I never have to worry about is becoming addicted to weed or anything else. I have a healthy fear of how it all affects my head. Even legal drugs, can't stand that feeling of being out of control or lifeless and lethargic.

6/16/97
Journal Entry

Washed and conditioned my hair last night. Decided to wear it natural, trying to get away from chemicals. Eventually, I plan to get it twisted for locks. Loving my natural right now, it's nice and full and feels fabulous!

When I got in last night, I smoked part of that same joint, made a hamburger and fries and watched TV. That Steve Harvey is hilarious. He had double episodes, both were re-runs but they still very funny! Then there was a decent movie on ABC about a woman who lost her memory after finding out her husband molested her daughter. The doctors called it a type of temporary hysterical thing which a person will utilize as a defense mechanism to avoid an intolerable situation. She really couldn't remember anything and her husband proceeded to weave a web of lies. He convinced her that not only had she killed her child in an accident, but also, her mother! Meanwhile, he was feeding her a drug, Halcion, to keep her 'out of it.'

Later:

Got through another day. Linda (my co-worker) and I went to Home Depot at lunch-time. She found two gorgeous plants at a cool price and we browsed around. She also bought a fifty-pound bag of rocks for two dollars. I started to get a bag for Paul but thought better of it since I'm not driving. We then went by her house and she showed me her lovely garden. You never know about a person. I never would have thought of Linda as someone who would take the time and effort to create and tend to a garden. At work she's always moving about franticly and snapping people up! Who knew? But now that I think about it, no one would guess this about Paul either. We have lots of luscious plants all over the apartment which he tends to lovingly, visitors always assume I'm the plant lover and are taken aback when Paul quickly makes it clear that it's him. Calls himself the Plant Doctor.

Afterwards, we went to Churches Chicken in the West End and bought hot wings and took them back to the office. Someone had bought bagels and cream cheese and sat them out on a tray. We didn't do much work after that.

Got lots of compliments on my hair. Linda was the exception.

"I hate it," she said. 'Hate' was a strong word for someone else's hairstyle, I thought.

"Why," I asked, not really caring, but curious and knowing she was going to tell me.

"Because your face is really round and that style really brings that out," she snapped. I think sometimes she's surprised that I don't react more strongly to some of the things she says like others around the office. They often take offense and usually allow her plenty of space. But I like her, she's harmless. Shoots straight from the hip. People like her are refreshing to me, I'm more relaxed around them, even though they can be irritating. We're just office buddies mostly and we sometimes walk together during lunch. She's a Jehovah's Witness. We've had some interesting talks and---oh yeah, her husband is an alcoholic and has health issues so guess we've got a lot in common.

Paul had fried Cod and cut potatoes for French fries when I got home. I made myself a salad. Everything was good but I left most of the potatoes, really trying to cut back on the fried stuff.

6/18/97
Journal Entry

These young brothers... I tell you! Here they are now on the train with their ear-phones, rapping loudly, cursing and flailing around. Just being obnoxious. No regard for others on the train. What the hell is wrong with them? I know they're young and want to have fun, but don't they ever think about anyone else? I just wish that I could see them doing something else, showing concern about something worthwhile, which I'm sure they do, but I'd like to SEE it. Here they are laughing at people, being rude and loud and disrespectful. Just teenagers, black and white, you know. They all love to piss off the adults. Usually, the driver will make them calm down, but not this one. Sometimes they're afraid.

Now here's this young sister-girl cracking her gum like an idiot. Where do these people come from? These are my people but I don't know them, you know. Is it me!?

6/19/97
Journal Entry

Morning, G. It's nice and cool this morning, but the prediction is for another hot one.

I baked a chicken breast and ate it with a slice of honey-wheat bread when I got home, yesterday evening. Topped that off with two glasses of orange juice while watching the last half of a sci-fi flick, 'Buried Alive Again II.' Then I went to bed and fell asleep immediately. Paul was already asleep on the sofa as I sat down to eat. I left him there, turned off the air and locked the patio doors. Before passing out, I murmured a short prayer. "Thanks for all the good in my life and thanks that Paul is safe and at home." Amen.

6/24/97
Journal Entry

Morning, G

On my way in. It's hot and humid. It was eighty-nine degrees yesterday and will only get hotter today.

Paul wasn't home when I got in yesterday. He still hasn't come in. I don't know what I'm feeling, but I didn't sleep much last night which I attribute to the heat as much as anything.

Betty Shabazz died yesterday. After suffering through three weeks of skin grafts from severe burns, she succumbed. What a sad thing! My heart is heavy.

This bus is certainly cool, thank goodness. Now the train is cool as well.

Yesterday, Joan Johnson told me that many of the people in her neighborhood are going to the Mike Tyson/Evander Holyfield fight. They're going to support Holyfield, he's from that area in College Park. Their tickets are two hundred dollars each. I'm proud of them! A seat in front of the TV is the best seat in the house! Of course, I'm not really a fan of boxing… not since Mohammed Ali.

Later:

Called Georgia State earlier and discussed work hours with Richard in Personnel. He agreed that I can do eight hours on weekends. I was prepared to quit, but I'm going to hang in there for now. Every little bit helps, G.

6/25/97
Journal Entry

On my way home. Enjoyed the class. Oh, I forgot to mention that I'm taking this Creative Writing class. Just something to do. You know I have to stay busy to keep my mind away from my personal problems. With this new class, the book club, the weekend gig at Georgia State and my regular gig, I may be slightly over-loaded, however.

It's been raining and now it's muggier than ever! That's Atlanta for you.

This brother just got on the train smelling really fowl. Man is that hard to take in this heat! I already don't feel well, geez! Going to shower and relax in bed when I get in.

Nita dropped me off at Georgia State today. She is hilarious. I would really like to see her pass the Bar. I told her so today for the umpteenth time. She didn't want to hear it.

"How long did you go to school to get your law degree?" I asked.

"All together, about seven years," she said. We've had this conversation before. She has a good position as a trainer in Staff Development with our agency that she really loves. She says she feels no pressure, except maybe disappointing her parents. They would like to see her practice law after spending all that money.

6/26/97

I stopped writing yesterday in a panic. There was an accident on Campbellton Road near Wells St. Police cars were everywhere, some of them had exited the vehicles and were wandering around in the woods that surround the apartment complex on the corner. Others were busy trying to usher the crowd further back from the scene. A young man on the bus said to no one in particular, "They found a body in the woods down there." Two female passengers gasped. A woman in front of me asked if it was a man or a woman. She held her hands tightly against her chin as if she was going to pray.

The young man shrugged indifferently," Don't know, I just caught snatches of it on the news on the radio before I left work." He didn't bother to look in the woman's direction. Without warning, my breathing became short and my stomach did a flip-flop. A body, oh my Lord, I hadn't seen Paul in about three days and he still wasn't answering the phone before I left work. He sometimes hangs in this area! Please let him be home when I get there! My thoughts were racing. I tried to calm down…like they say, don't claim it. But it was no use. I couldn't shake the fear. Then … I saw the feet of a woman who was lying on a stretcher on the street. Her upper body was covered. I couldn't tell if she'd been thrown from the car or if she was hit by it. I could see white sandals on her feet and her dress looked like blue denim, I could only see the bottom of it. Suddenly I was so tired. It wasn't Paul, I thought, relieved. Then I felt ashamed. That poor woman…

The bus is loud. Kids are everywhere. People standing all over the place, thrown against each other as the bus jerked into moving traffic. Kids crying. The motor is loud, LOUD!

Paul was in bed snoring loudly when I got home. I could see that he'd actually showered and put on fresh pajamas.

6/27/97
Journal Entry

I'm at Georgia State waiting for the writing class to begin.
Today was crazy! Haven't felt well all day. Not really sick but just generally sluggish. Things went wrong first thing this morning when my computer began acting up. When I phoned Paris Systems Programs for help, I was told, to my dismay, that this particular problem had been going on for three days but because no one had made them aware of it until today, they would have to do the repairs on the weekend. In short, I would not be able to do any data entry today. And Monday is the last day of the month! Are you kidding me? Talk about pressure! I went on and completed most of the other work that I could. When Nita suggested going out for lunch, I was the first one on the bandwagon. We went to Red Lobster, mainly because Nita wanted a Pina Colada. I decided on a Long Island Tea, which surprisingly had plenty of liquor in it. Lunch was good and we laughed and clowned around as usual. Only problem was we didn't get back to the office until after 3:00 o'clock again. We were warned the moment we entered the building that Mandy had been looking for us and was pretty upset. Of course, this was an exaggeration, but she was a bit perturbed. Apparently, a couple of walk-in clients had come in and no one was available to see them. We felt bad. After all, Mandy had told us the last time that she didn't mind us taking an extended lunch occasionally as long as we brought it to her attention before-hand, which was more than generous. I felt like a grade-school kid.

Later:

Man am I tired. Ms. Brown returned my poems tonight.

"I didn't write anything on them," she said. I was disappointed. After entering the hallway, I turned and went back.

"I didn't mind you writing on them, I was hoping you'd critique them," I said.

She still refrained from commenting on the quality but showed some interest in my poem 'Trees.' She pointed out a couple of words she'd leave out. She made sense.

There's a couple near the back of the bus arguing about how long they've been riding. A young girl is holding the cutest little toddler. The child's shoes are off and she's giggling and playing with her toes in wonder. Kids... God, I love them!

Forgot to tell you that I finally checked out that bakery downtown that my co-workers have been raving about, 'The Heavenly Fathers' Bakery,' it's called. It's down there near Five Points. This elderly black sister was loudly preaching and praising God when I entered.

"The God I serve don't let me worry about nothin,' and I don't have to steal, cheat and scheme," she bellowed.

"Amen," I said, knowing the response she wanted. "What kind of whole cakes do you have and how much are they," I asked.

"The Heavenly Lemon and the Heavenly Plain Cake, sista. The Heavenly Lemon is thirteen dollars and the Heavenly Plain is twelve dollars, sista. Yeah, people may not love me, praise the Lord, but I love all of them, sista. The God I serve don't care about no racism or nothin' like that."

"Amen," I said. Give me a slice of your chocolate there and a piece of the Banana Nut Bread, please."

"That'll be three dollars and seventy-five, sista, praise the Lord."

I can't recall her name but if you ever try her pastries, you'll be inclined to believe every word she says. Her counter-top and the walls behind it are covered with scripture. She's light-tanned and loud, Lord she's loud. She was dressed in all-white garb from head to toe, her head was covered, like a Muslim or a Nun. As she praises the Lord, she leans back on her legs and throws her head back and belts out each word.

"Yes, Lord, to know Him is to be released from Fear. When you come to love, Fear is gone, sista. Ain't that right, brotha?" A slight, thin man had entered. He was standing there with a little boy, probably his son. The boys' eyes were shining in anticipation of the delicious pastries.

"That's right, the man said, smiling timidly.

She dropped the large chunks of cake in a plain white bag, then threw in two other items without fan-fare. I knew better than to comment other than to say simply, "thank you so much." She'd already dismissed me and was giving the slender man and his son her full attention. She began her praises all over again as I left. A large group of young white professionals entered behind me. I had to chuckle--- sister-girl had a great location and business was booming in the heart of downtown Atlanta, praise the Lord!

I didn't look into the bag until I boarded the train. She'd thrown in a huge chunk of Pudding cake (Heavenly, of course) and another huge piece of Heavenly Brownie Cake. It was difficult not to bite into at least one of these delicacies while on the train, the smell alone almost made me swoon, I was so hungry! I delighted myself later that evening. Each treat was wonderful and she was overly generous with the portions. There was more than enough for me and Paul. I carefully tucked away a little for myself, knowing Paul would devour it all once he tasted it and he would have a ready excuse for me, "I thought you'd left this for me! Ha! Yeah, right!

7/8/97
Journal Entry

Traveling to work:

Very trying weekend. All I can do is pray. In so much emotional pain. The rent is short, I'm struggling to come up with the money. I wrote a check anyway! I'm angry. Paul has really been in a bad way. He promised to give me money so that we could handle it, but what did he do? Blew all of his money in the streets. He was gone from Tuesday morning until Friday. Came in sick as all get out. One side of his face was swollen and he was obviously in a lot of pain. Don't exactly know what happened to him but he refused to go to the hospital. He managed to eat something and then lay down on the sofa. There was only silence between us. Then yesterday morning he jumped up, took a shower and was out the door, mumbling something about VA hospital. If he'd gone to the hospital, I would've heard something by now. Like I said, I'm in continuous prayer.

Later:

Well, I was denied the loan. One of those little rip-off companies downtown. Seven-hundred dollars, for God's sake! On the upside (if there is such a thing), I didn't have a lot of time to brood about it. I was on Intake today and had to interview all day, non-stop. Guess that's what's called a productive day, working hard, not having time to dwell on personal problems. That's one thing I've always been able to do, when I'm working, I engross myself in my work, I love what I do in spite of the stress. But I'm not sure I understand anything anymore. There is too much going on. I put one-hundred and sixty-six dollars in the bank, all I had. Don't ask me what good it's going to do. I truly need a financial blessing!

Don't know why this bus is just sitting. Normally, the #83 will pull off as soon as we board in the evening. Here we go, now we're moving. It's not unbearably hot now, but it's still hot.

I know I'm going to regret writing the rental check. It's going to be costly. Don't even want to think about the repercussions right now. And in retrospect, why didn't I hold on to the cash? It's just going to be eaten up in fees, the checks no good. I'm not thinking at all!

There are some nice homes in this area off of Campbellton Road. You wouldn't believe it. I'd love to get one of these or one in the Cascade area. But there's many nice areas to check out when the time is right.

7/9/97
Journal Entry

Haven't seen Paul since Tuesday morning. No phone call, nothing. I pray he's okay.

Got a lot of organizing to do this morning. Then writing class tonight. Last night I completed a poem for the Campbell Soup contest. Today, I'll give it as well as my editorial letter to Essence Magazine, to Cathy to type for me.

It's going to be another hot one. The prediction is at least eighty-seven degrees. Just boarded this crowded train. Folks staring as I write, as usual.

Hope to hear something from Paul. If he's okay, it's so unfair for him not to at least make contact.

Later:

Class was good tonight. Gwen Brown really knows how to get you motivated. She's not overly critical but she will let you know just what you need to do. She's passionate.

"Explore, investigate, dig down deep, and then write about it," she says. She won't allow you to apologize for what you've written, either. There's lots of talent in this class, I think everyone in here is sincere. A few of them have published poetry, short stories, etc, in the past. They all continue coming. Most are coming from work as I do and we arrive early. Most come by train, which is very convenient because the train runs directly into Georgia State University.

Everyone loved my poem 'Momma.' I read it aloud and someone exclaimed how well-written it was, got lots of positive feed-back. It felt good. Gwen Brown wants everyone to submit their work somewhere.

7/10/97
Journal Entry

Rode into work with Della this morning. She lives just up the hill in my apartment complex. We arrived to work on time in spite of the slow traffic on Lakewood Freeway.

At eight-thirty, a nurse from Grady Hospital called.

"Is this June Calloway?"

"Yes, I said. I could hardly breathe.

"This is Grady Memorial Hospital calling regarding Paul Calloway."

"Yes, is he alright?" I held my breath.

"Mr. Calloway is here at the hospital and will soon be transported to Georgia Regional Hospital. He asked me to call you and let you know."

"IS HE ALRIGHT?" I tried not to scream.

"Yes, he's okay. That's all she had for me.

"Well, thanks for calling me, then," I said. I truly was grateful. To be honest, G, the staff at Grady knows him almost as well as the VA staff. They've admitted him many times after one of his binges and kept him over-night instead of putting him back out on the street. They know about his disabilities, his paranoia and dehydration and all the meds he takes, all that. Usually, they will transport him to VA the next day for further treatment. Often, some compassionate nurse will lecture him about his life-threatening life style before he leaves. These people are angels, G, just like you.

During the day, I didn't try to call Georgia Regional, I know that he was transferred there for mental evaluation and to make sure he isn't suicidal. It's too early in the game. If he doesn't call this evening, I'll call there. I'm very concerned for him at this point, but I'm thankful that he's hospitalized. Beyond that, it's hard for me to think about him, let alone communicate with him.

7/12/97
Journal Entry

I t's Thursday and I just got off. I'm so thankful to spend an evening at home.

We had a meeting this afternoon. Barbara Johnson wanted to get feed-back from us regarding all the changes and the new Intake procedures. There was plenty of griping and complaining as usual. But further into the meeting, there was some positive ideas. Several suggestions were made which the Management Team agreed to look into and address at a later date.

Our assignment from yesterdays' writing class is to get or at least familiarize ourselves with Haiku Poetry (Japanese Poetry) and complete a Nature poem (whatever that is). I'll have to get to the library tomorrow before I visit Paul. I'll have to write the poem sometime tomorrow. Paul is in the VA hospital, by the way, G. He was transferred from Georgia Regional and I'm thankful. He's more comfortable and he gets good care. Tonight, I'm going to relax, clean the apartment, start my budget, call Paul and my Mom. Can't forget to call the utility companies to make bill payment arrangements as soon as possible, too. Have to plan.

There was a man who appeared out of nowhere at Five Points Station, right in front of the Bar next to the store. He strutted over toward the door carrying a Boom-Box. A white scarf draped his neck and he wore black leather pants and shirt. His face was heavily made up and his hair was slicked back. Didn't have a tooth in his mouth!

"Hey, looka he-a!" He dropped the Boom-Box next to the door. It was booming. He broke out into a funky James Brown-slide. The Box blared, "Papa don't, Poppa don't, Poppa don't take no mess." He sang along, red gums gleaming. He was gettin' down! He slid from one edge of the store to the next. With another 'James Brown' scream, he danced with everything he had. People exiting Five Points and others coming and going from all directions, stopped in their tracks to admire him. Someone yelled, "The hardest working man in show business" and the crowd laughed and clapped. Then someone yelled, "Go head, go head!" The crowd picked it up. It was hilarious, I had to stop, the spontaneity was contagious! The crowd from the restaurant had gathered outside. They seemed to know him and yelled, "Go head, James!"

7/18/97
Journal Entry

I'm out here again. Right now I'm headed east on the train to the VA to see Paul.

Gail called me last night. I was sipping on some Courvoisier and cooking fresh string beans. I'd planned to do some cleaning, but it just wasn't in me. Once I got in, turned on the air and fixed my cocktail, I barely had energy to prepare dinner. Gail wanted to know what she'd missed after she left the book-club meeting. I filled her in. We laughed about what had gone on before she left. I hung up and ate. It was useless watching TV. I'd tried to reach Paul several times, but the line stayed busy. As soon as I nodded out in front of the TV, he called. He complained about a mix-up in his medication. Said his blood-pressure was rising. He wasn't in pain but wanted me to know what was going on. They wouldn't give him anything for it.

Later:

Paul has gotten his hair cut. He looks like a different person. He had his exam this morning and feels positive about it. Say's the doctor is a 'sista' and she seemed compassionate and asked him relevant questions.

Headed downtown now. I've got time to stop at the main library and find a Japanese Poetry book. I've got about three hours before class. Don't know if I can complete or even conceive of a poem in time but I'm going to give it a shot. Poetry comes easy to me. There's no struggle involved, it's like I visualize the words flashing in my head when I attempt a poem and sometimes it's as if someone is dictating words to me. I actually enjoy it! Yet, I don't consider myself a poet and I don't write it very often even though I've had several poems published. Go figure!

These brothers walk around here and they barely weigh a hundred pounds. Know they're on drugs. It's crazy! I know I shouldn't judge.

Later:

At Five Points Station. There's a young man with a Boom-box blasting a rap song about "bitches and ho's! Madness! He's sitting there, stoned out of his head, oblivious to his surroundings. Everyone's looking embarrassed, black, white and brown, avoiding eye contact.

Writing class was good. We had a guest speaker. Her name was Falami 'something.' I'm terrible with names. She read some fantastic poetry and shared her thoughts about the importance of diversity. This is something I don't hear many black women talking about in the mainstream. But she spoke my thoughts. She also gave us a list of books on literature, poetry and biographies. Definitely plan to get some of them.

Betty read her poem about a black woman which spanned several centuries. Shane, a white brother, read his piece about teenaged pregnancies, and Harold did one about a woman who grew old and never followed her dream to become a doctor, and although she'd had a good life, she was saddened in her old-age. It was great! Gwen Brown pointed out some minor errors in each but said that over-all, our work was moving and powerful. How about that?

The bus driver and some guy is arguing up front. Oh, Lord!

"I work hard for mine, and just did fifteen years. What you need to do is just do your job," he shouted. Apparently, she'd made a comment when he boarded. She had stopped for him after she'd taken off. She didn't have to but she did. Anyway, he didn't appreciate her comment. Thankfully, she went quiet. Things could have gone from zero to ten in a New York minute. You never know who's going to go off, never know who you're talking to out here!

7/21/97
Journal Entry

Morning, G. I'm excited about reading my poem Wednesday evening.

It's cloudy and humid already. Apparently, there's going to be plenty of rain as a result of Hurricane Danny. Well, actually, Danny's been down-graded to a tropical storm, but it's going to cause torrents of rain here, in Alabama and surrounding areas. Here comes the rain now.

7/22/97
Journal Entry

I'm exhausted. It was extremely humid last night. It had cooled down somewhat after the rain, but it was sticky. When I got into bed, the sheets stuck to me, I almost felt feverish. I gave up and closed the windows and turned on the air. Let it run all night which I hate doing because the bill is high as all get out already. I woke up freezing, but as soon as I began moving around, I felt the heat.

There's a seventeen year old missing from College Park. Pretty young girl. News reports says she was on her way to a summer job which she'd just gotten three days before. She left that third morning going to the bus-stop. She never made it to work. No one has seen her.

Later:

Completed Intake cases all day today. This train is packed. I get a few stares as I write as usual.

Atlanta has such a lovely sky-line. The sun's returned and it's cooler out. According to the news, Alabama is drenched due to the storm.

I'm going to eat light tonight, salad and maybe eggs or something.

7/24/97
Journal Entry

Greyhound Bus Terminal
Wow, what a morning! Taxi was late, I missed the Huntsville bus, actually it was there when I arrived, but took off as I purchased my ticket, had to wait for the next one.

Paul was released from VA hospital yesterday, but he never came home. Oh well, he's in the Creator's hands. I've got to go.

Here I am at the station with another hour to kill. I'm ravenous but I refuse to purchase this awful, expensive food (I've tried it before). People are milling around looking anxious, some appear bored. Others are sleeping. 'Sanford and Son' reruns are blaring on the large-screen TVs.

A man stands in the middle of the place near customer service, profiling, as we use to say. Well dressed, good-looking, demanding attention. A young pregnant white woman, dingy white Tee shirt, stringy blond hair stands to my left arguing with an older man. A white brother steps up and offers me a light for my cigarette. There's a young Spanish family at the next table, four little restless, irritable children. She had to spend a fortune for all the food she bought for them. Tacos with a lot of gook, cookies and cake.

7/28/97
Journal Entry

Made it home from Alabama in one piece this morning at six am. It was rough going and coming, G, but the in-between was wonderful. I watched my son walk across the stage and accept his degree in Special Education. All the hassle was worthwhile. Amen.

7/29/97
Journal Entry

Paul woke me up at six-thirty am. If he hadn't, I would've really over-slept. It's hard for me to get to sleep with this humidity, then it's hard to wake up once I get to sleep. Sleeping under the air does a job on my sinuses, causing my head to ache.

"You can't depend on me for these things anymore. This new medication I'm taking makes me feel like I've been put under sedation," said Paul.

"Did you make coffee?"

"I just started a pot."

He started going on and on about current events, I could tell he was feeling pretty good.

"A black man in Decatur, Georgia, won Sixty Million in the lotto. He's sixty-five years old and retired. Goddam! You've got to play, you know… only way you're gonna win! Bill Cosby's decided to take a test to determine if he's the father of that girl. He's concerned about the court of public opinion. Old as he is and as much money as he's got, I don't know why he'd give a damn. What's he gonna prove? People love him that love him. He might even prove that the girl's mother's been lying all these years. The girl is pretty as hell! But I think he's going to wind up hurting himself. It's ridiculous!"

He was beside me in the bathroom mirror, now.

"Get out, I'm trying to get ready for work," I said. He ignored me.

"Man, if I'd kept doing what I was doing, we would've branched out by now. We'd have a place in Warren, all around the area. And especially if I'd stayed in politics. I'd have Danny running shit. I'd be down in Washington doing my thing. They'd be talking about me like I was Newt Gingrich. He got there interest up there in Ohio! I wouldn't give a fuck. I'd run from DC to Ohio. Let Danny run the shit, you know?"

"You need to stop," I said.

"Yeah, I've got to stop dwelling on the past, what could have been. Got to deal with what's happening now. Yeah, man, like I said before, that dude up at the VA hospital got it going on. And he might be doing his thing for free. I know he's retired. Might be making some money, but then again, he may not be getting anything. Always smiling. You can tell he enjoys what he's doing. And the dudes be standing in line to see him. He helps them handle their grievances, a patient advocate, I guess, don't know if that's his title or what. I could get into that. It's cool. Doing something to help the people. Don't care what no one says, I want to help the people."

Later:

Made another day. Went well, G. I was thankful Mandy wasn't there when I got to the office this morning. It was after seven and her door was closed, which usually means she's in there. Turns out someone had closed it for some reason. She didn't show up until around ten-thirty. I've got to do better.

Paul called me in the afternoon and said that Gwen Brown had called me. She'd tried to reach me at the office. I tried to reach her at the library where she worked with no luck. But on a positive tip, I got a flash of confidence about speaking with her and imagined her telling me that someone had an interest in my poems. I tried to suppress my exhilaration at the thought. Then I spoke to my higher power: "G, I accept all the good that's for me without reservation. I repeated this to myself. It really made me feel good. It's just as easy to feel positive about my work as it is to feel fearful, you see.

7/31/97
Journal Entry

My morning started out well. Got up at five-twenty am, did some crunches, made coffee and showered.

When Paul woke up, we had an emotional discussion concerning the bills and finances. In a sense, we both won. We'll see tomorrow. I'll have to do what I always suggest he do... put my faith in action.

Later: On train going home.

This clown next to me says out of the blue, "You got any hand-lotion?" He has an accent, obviously African or from one of the islands. I mention this because a regular brother would never approach a sister on the train this way! On the train? No, baby. Seriously, a conscious brother or even the lowliest brother wouldn't do this, just too un-cool! His hands are rough and ashy and I assume he's just left some physical job. But still... as I write this he's still determined to talk to me, knowing he's already irritated me. Why do people confront you like that?! Just no boundaries whatsoever!

"It amazes me to watch some one left-hand write. And you have beautiful handwriting." He smiled, revealing one huge yellow tooth. Instantly, I felt sorry for this young man. I'm not sure why. But he's young and polite and struggling to survive in a culture not his own, in this city 'too busy to hate' as they say, ha! I've paid some dues here and I can easily empathize with many of the black folk in this city, I've seen my share of hate, racism and suffering...

We're approaching Green Briar Mall. I'll stop at the Food Court and get some Rib Tips. There's beer at the house. All right! This is my chill-out night and I'm off tomorrow, yeah!

Man, I tell you I can feel what it is to own a home already. Taking pride in something of your own. Neighborhood groups showing concern for the neighborhood and each other. It's a whole different world. My world. Living as one should. Not from pay to pay, sky-high rent, few amenities, small rooms. I could cry if I added up all the rent I've paid... we've paid. I did this a couple years ago and got depressed. Said I wouldn't do that to myself again. Unbelievable!

8/4/97
Journal Entry

It's Monday and I'm on my way to a two-day training session for the TANF program. We're supposed to get new information and guidelines. But it's probably more of the same gobbledygook.

Did I mention that great time I had last week at Keith's graduation? Now that he has his degree, he can sign the contract and begin teaching in September, he's already substituted for the past two years. I'm so proud of him. We had a tremendous amount of food, Carol and I cooked until times got better. I was also impressed by the number of friends that gathered at their home afterwards. Two of his uncles were there and I thanked them for their support for the past few years.

Right now, I'm tired, hungry, stomach is irritated and really, I don't feel up to sitting with a room full of colleagues, listening to some bureaucrat telling me how much 'more' work I've got to do. More than likely I'm going to fall asleep. Also, I'm concerned about finances right now. I'm trusting in you, G (my guide) that you will appeal to the author, the Supreme Author, to help with this particular script. I submit fully. Amen, Sela!

The writers' group meeting is tomorrow. Yeah, a few of us started a group after the class at Georgia State ended. I haven't written anything since then. Got to get on the stick.

Now this same speaker is talking about what retirement's going to be like. She's well invested, according to her. Talking about having to work for McDonald's after retirement, or being in one of those K-mart commercials, etc. All this reminds me, I need to call the Retirement Board and check on my individual retirement situation.

Okay, they're starting to return from lunch. Jerry and some guy who resembles a TV personality (can't remember who, exactly) have returned. They're both trainers.

I've got to start my budget. Also need to write something for class. Then again, maybe I'll just take something that I already have.

8/5/97
Journal Entry

Good morning, G. It's a wonderful morning. I'm feeling thankful and very grateful. Your wonderful Spirit is moving in our lives. I can see and feel it. Right now I'm marveling at the renewed animation in Pauls' attitude. Your ways are a mystery to us, but your way is natural. You see the entire picture. You know the whole story. You know what's true. You know our needs. We are weak but You are strong. Your Spirit is ageless, timeless and hip, even! You have an answer for all time. We thank You for your Holy Mercy and Grace! I could go on and on. The look of hope and desire to be understood, to make amends, is all there in his eyes. I claim it. It's here and we're ready for it. We accept it with all praises and thanks. We are ready to do Your Will. We recognize that ultimately Your Will is the only will and that it is One with ours. Thanks so much in the name of Jesus Christ.

I don't mean to sound phony and 'holier than thou.' I don't mean to go overboard because I know I don't begin to have any answers. But I know that You do and if You are for us, who can be against us? I know that we can look forward to positive changes. We accept them even in our fear, Lord. We know that fear is unnatural and untrue. We move now past the fear. This is my prayer and my intercessory prayer for Paul as well. Amen.

When I came home yesterday, Paul was sitting up, clean, calm and in good spirits. He began talking to me in an animated and warm voice about the VA hospital. There was not the usual trace of anger, in fact, he was mostly humorous and good-natured as he spoke and shared with me for more than two hours. I listened attentively. This is something we haven't done in a very long time. I'm feeling amazed that in the last several days, the light seems to have come on!

Later: Lunch

I brought a piece of pizza from home, thank goodness. Heated it in the micro-wave on the second floor. Judy, from Staff Development, directed me toward the coffee only to discover that there was none. I just polished off the pizza and a bottle of water. Now I'm outside, smoking. Feels really good out here. Air-conditioning takes its' toll on a body after a while.

This training session is quite interesting. They've apparently put some policy in order and procedures seem more clear, however, in spite of my former supervisor's sense of humor, she is quite irritating, with her little games she's devised to get us up out of our seats and moving, etc. Her intentions are supposed to lift morale. Right.

I'm back in the Conference room. Most of my colleagues haven't returned from lunch yet. There's a nice-looking dark-skinned sister sitting near the back who appears about my age. She's going on about not sending any more children to a black college. Says she's run into many problems with two children in college (black, I assume). Says there are empty buildings that aren't utilized for the students. She believes the administrators are lining their pockets. She goes on to talk about her credentials as a former teacher and board member.

Training has resumed, now they're discussing retirement, when one can retire, etc.

8/6/97
Journal Entry

No one has to lose for me to gain. I accept the abundance of the Universe knowing that there is enough for me. I have all that I need. I am rich! Selah.

On my way in to work. Writers' group tonight, forgot to bring my poems. It's just as well. Just getting there is the important thing. Being with the other writers is important for me right now. Whatever else is accomplished will just 'happen.'

I can't believe I've been in this city for eleven years. Amazing how time passes. As I ride the train, I'm reminded of the places I've lived and hung out, etc.

I think I just irritated the guy next to me with all of my stuff... radio, notebook, umbrella, purse, lunch, ridiculous, hahaha!

Later:

What a day! I worked non-stop from nine-thirty until four-forty pm. No breaks except for a cigarette. No lunch, just interviews. Upon arriving at work, I discovered I was on Intake. Never mind my Production Report was due. Had to reschedule three applications for tomorrow. Never mind that I have five TANF reviews scheduled already. I was super busy and due to hunger, I became irritable. Decided not to attend the Writers' meeting tonight. Too tired.

Brenda, a colleague from Child Support Services gave me a Marta Card which is good through Sunday. We were just talking and I happened to ask if she had change for a ten-dollar bill so that I could catch the train.

"No, I don't have change but if you need it for the train, I've got an extra Marta Card—here, you can have it."

"Oh, really, you won't get into any trouble, will you? I asked.

"Hey, girl, I need my job. Wouldn't do anything to jeopardize it, okay? But we've got to look out for one another, you know?"

"Ha ha! That's right, girl-friend. I really appreciate this. Thanks a lot. When did you start staying until five-thirty?" I asked.

"This is my first week. I'm on Marta too, you know. I bought a little house six months ago. Nothing fancy. A little brick house. Needs a lot of fixing up. But I'm just doing a little at a time, you know. So my car blew up on me a few weeks ago. It was an old car, raggedy as hell, you know what I mean? It blew up on me! Girl, I can't afford no new car payments. A close friend of mine just bought some kind of little jeep. Her payments are six hundred dollars a month! That's a house-payment, for me, you know what I mean? I can't handle it. So right now, I'm staying on the train."

I silently marveled. I was going through the same thing. Only I hadn't gotten a house yet. Still trying to get one. Had found out that I could qualify easier without a new car payment. So here I was without the house or car. But it was looking good. I didn't have time to tell her all of this. It was five-thirty and I still had to clear my desk. But it gave me a renewed sense of respect for her as well as kinship. I'd already decided that she was cool based on the way I'd seen her interact with her clients. Once, a few weeks ago, I'd gone to her with a question: My client is now working and in need of a Marta Transit Card." She could have told me to have my client go through the normal procedure of getting placed on a list and waiting several hours, but she didn't.

"We need to assist those who are willing to work, don't you think?" Of course, I agreed with her.

My day went much smoother than yesterday. My trainee came in at nine and I promptly put her to work putting my Manual Transmittal

Letters in order, filing closed cases and opening mail. She even pulled up the print for the closures after I showed her the basics. She's definitely a keeper. Only one of the Intakes from yesterday showed up today and only two scheduled TANF's showed up, however, I still didn't get a chance to complete my Production report. Got to get in early tomorrow and get it done.

Paul wasn't home when I called this afternoon. I'm not going to read anything into that, though. It's a little premature. Hope he didn't get caught in the rain. It was raining torrents around three o'clock.

8/7/97
Journal Entry

S ee, it pays to try and keep negativity at bay and think in the affirmative. Paul came home yesterday a little after eight, says he didn't get out of VA until after five. Don't know if he attended an NA meeting or what afterwards but he certainly was UP when he came home. He's impressed with his new therapist. He says she listens, she's competent and she's very nice. Says she apparently knows her shit.

TGIF! I certainly have my weekend cut out for me if I do what I should. Get the apartment clean and do some writing for the most part.

They're still widening the street on Campbellton Road from Delowe Dr. to Timothy St. No telling when they'll complete it. I'm going to be late this morning. Hope it doesn't rain today. Didn't bring my umbrella.

I'm confident that I can complete a book of poetry without fan-fare. Writing about things that are relevant in my life; communication, relationships, spirituality, friendships, family, addictions, fear, etc., that's easy. The craftsmanship with which I'm able to say something meaningful about these things is what matters the most.

Later:

There's a brother sitting in front of me with a white linen suit on, with a pink straw hat with a black band around it. A yellow feather in the band. As he sat down, the hem hung loose from his jacket.

I must release myself from this fatigue. Get a good nights' sleep. Drink some milk. Eat some vegetables.

I can tell they've done some work on these apartments on Campbellton Road. Particularly these two we're passing... Briar House and Regal Heights. These two actually look decent now.

8/12/97
Journal Entry

Morning, G. Please permit me to say it with ease. Paul has changed. For the better. He walked to the bus stop with me this morning. We split a pack of cigarettes. He gave a homeless guy two.

"I can't just turn my head and pretend I don't see him. I've been out there myself. You know what I mean?" Yeah, I knew what he meant. He scowled at a well-dressed sister who ignored the man when he asked her for a dollar. "Now see, she just looked right past him. As if he wasn't there. That's wrong. Sometimes, it's the little things that are so cruel, man!"

Evening:

Made another day. My sisters will be here day after tomorrow on Thursday. I'll probably crash tonight before I do anything. I'm exhausted and in need of rest but I do need to clean do some cleaning and shopping.

Folks on the train give you the strange eye often. If you take it personal, it will make you paranoid. By all means do not give anyone your full attention (unless, of course, you feel the need to extend some positive energy and blessings to a particular individual that may hone in on your radar, I don't fully understand these things but, trust me, they happen, I've experienced it), you do not want to feel their crazy… seriously.

This high-yellow brother next to me is trying real hard to get my attention. He complimented me on my left-handed writing. I smiled and continued writing, hoping to avoid a conversation.

It's hot and humid as usual. I see women wiping perspiration from their brow, unusual for Atlanta women, I rarely see them perspire. It's just SO hot! Guess that's why it's called 'Hot Lanta!'

Some of these new short hair-cuts I'm checking out on my black sisters are really slamming! Got me thinking.

I'm so sleepy and hot, can't wait to get home.

8/13/97

L ast night was an experience. A brother from 'Come an' Rent (a rent to own company that I rented a washer and dryer from) came to the house after 10:00 pm! He banged on the door until Paul answered and told him I wasn't home. I became incensed and raised the upstairs window, explaining to him that I'd already arranged payment with one of the managers and that it was next to my last payment. I got nowhere. He insisted I give him a payment right then. He also had some choice words for Paul!

"Why don't you come out and face me like a man?" At this point Paul stepped outside. They argued. Won't tell you all that was said. Paul tried to reason with him but it got ugly! The brother exclaimed, "I have a goddam MBA!

"Man, apparently, you don't know who you're talking to," said Paul. He stopped short of telling him that he, too, has an MBA. I give him credit for that… he knows and accepts the fact that many of our people here in the ATL are different…just different from black folks in the North. Meanwhile, I'm livid! I'm wondering what in the world does an MBA have to do with the price of tea in China! Where is your black pride? Your sense of brotherhood? Where we're from, we take a stand for each other in these stupid ass situations, knowing there's little we can do to help you! But no, some of THESE black folk treat you worse than the white folk! You cannot reason with them. They will uphold the system/company with their life, while on a minimum wage job! Slave mentality, you know?

Paul was ready to kick his ass, I had to intervene.

Father, please help me to accept the things which I cannot change. I have joy and meaning in my life. My wealth comes independently of my position on the job. Paul has his sobriety and faith and he also has his mind back. Both of us are productive and happy. I speak these things into being. Amen.

8/14/97
Journal Entry

Made it today. It was tough, however. I was tired and irritable. My last client and I clashed big time! It was so weird… we got a really bad start, I'd just hung up from talking with Paul. It went on for a while until I threw my hands up and declared, "Can't help you, Bro. I'll find someone else to take care of you." Mr. Jones eventually interviewed him. He took him off of my system and everything.

My sisters got in this morning. Guess what? Their room wasn't ready. They didn't get into their suite until late this afternoon. Thank goodness, they're in a nice place, the Residence Inn. Joan just called before I left work. So now I'm on my way home and I can chill out while they go back to the hotel and do the same.

What a day! Can't believe how that guy went off on me. He really didn't make any effort to connect with me and I didn't help much, you know. That bothers me because I usually vibe pretty good with my clients.

Father, in You, I can go about my daily affairs in an exalted state. I can interact peacefully and courageously in all my physical contacts, I can lift my head joyously without concern over financial matters. I am a spiritual being. In You I always long to be. In You there is never a worry about what I will wear, what I will say, how I'll say it, where I will go, how much money I have, whatever anyone else has. How I look. What I will eat, how I am perceived, how I perceive. For all of this, I give thanks. I give You the Glory! Knowing that everything that there is belong to You in the first and last place. So be it.

I really can see myself being with April, Betty and Michael this evening. They love writing as much as I do. I thank the Creator for the gift of creation through writing. The ability to record my feelings and thoughts and the actions of others is a wondrous thing. A thing that connects me with Spirit. I pray that that this gift remains with me throughout my life.

Riding Marta gives one the unique opportunity to observe the people of the community, the every-day people who commute daily. These include some of Atlanta's well-to-do as well as the poorest of the poor. You will also recognize the many transplants from all over the country. Black, white and brown.

8/17/97

Morning, G
On my way to the Southwest Office for a seminar called 'Changing the Culture of Welfare." We've already seen this guy on video. He's pretty good. Again, there's nothing new under the sun, but if someone can come up with a more innovative or imaginative way of presenting it, it can still be interesting and exciting. So maybe this will not be a dull day. Might even pick up something worthwhile.

I love riding down through here in the Lynhurst Dr. and Cascade area. It is so scenic and refreshing, such beautiful homes. All black, mind you.

There's teenagers on the bus this morning, going to school, of course.

I know Gail had to be embarrassed yesterday. The thing is, she could have avoided it. We were in my office having a brief morning discussion when she noticed a fifty-dollar bill on my desk.

"Wow! I haven't seen one of those in a long time," she said, her eyes wide. Gail is always dramatic.

"Oh, come on, girl, I'm going to get coffee," I chuckled. "And, I've got to give Shadru twenty of those dollars. Believe me, I hate doing it. Usually, I try to keep my tab down to five or six bucks, but it got a little out of hand."

"Well, since you're going over there, take care of mine, will you? It's only a dollar or two," she added, nonchalantly.

"Sure," I said. She's done me favors (really baled me out big-time a couple of times), I didn't have a problem.

"Thanks, you know I'm good for it," she said.

"No problem, girl." I didn't think anything of it until I got to the cafeteria. After paying my bill, I asked Shadru, "How much is Ms. Steven's bill?"

"Gail's?" His brow went up and he scowled. "Why do you ask?"

"She asked me to take care of it for her." I smiled, growing a little uncomfortable.

"No, I want to see her," he said emphatically. She is playing games, you see. She's not right, you see." His irritation mounted and he waived his arms and stabbed the air with his fingertips and shook his head as he spoke. "Here, see, here is the bill. It is four dollars and seventeen cents! She gave me a check and it bounced!" He lowered his voice. "It is going to cost her!" His Pakistani accent thickened as his words rushed forth. "The bank will charge her twenty and I will charge her twenty-five because that is how much it cost me!" I held up my hand to stop him. "Shadru, I'm going to let her handle this. This is something for you and her to discuss." I was becoming irritated by now. The whole thing was so petty.

"It is all for six dollar, he yelled. She will pay forty-five dollar for six dollar check! She don't even have six dollar in her checking account! Disgusting!" He shook his head, incredulously, which made the whole thing kind of funny, I had to stifle myself from laughing. But I'd also heard more than I wanted to.

"I'll tell her you want to see her, Shadru."

He looked at me pleadingly. "Please, please do. Because she is a lady of games. This is the last, the very last time we deal with her. She is like scum!"

"You can discuss it with her," I said, walking away. "Scum, he called her. Wow! Before he'd bellowed that out, I was furious with Gail. But not so much now. I was embarrassed for her, realizing she'd been avoiding him. But 'scum! I know Gail's story. She moved here from South Carolina a few years ago after a crazy divorce, got a job with DFAC's and worked another part-time job for years. Purchased a home and a new car. A real go-getter...far from scum. So... these things happen. And the crazy thing is, knowing Shadru, he would give her credit again if it came down to it. He would not pass up a dollar.

8/28/97

Morning G

Thanks to the Most High! This is Thursday and the last day of work! Monday is Labor Day. This means I'll be off until next Tuesday.

Got a lot of work done yesterday. Today I'm on Intake which means there won't be time to do much else. At least I'm prepared. I do need to check on some cases---the ones that didn't return for an interview, these may have to be denied.

God's good fresh air sure feels good this morning. But it's supposed to reach ninety-five degrees later today.

Great plans for the weekend; walking in the mornings, watching movies and writing. First, of course, the bills must be taken care of. Paul says he's going to get through the weekend without any drugs. I'm trusting that the Creator will assist him in every way and that I will not interfere, consciously or subconsciously, okay Father? Your Will is our will. We know that Your Power is Almighty. I'm also trusting in You for Ransom's right-thinking and doing. I know that through You, he will endure and over-come. I'm committing myself to fifty dollars a month to send to put on his books (you know that he's incarcerated, right, G?). I know that You will help me follow through. Also, through You, his family/our family will communicate with him, write him and all. I don't know in fact how he feels but You know I feel his pain. He's my son. While I'm at it, thank you for my dear mother, she's my rock and thank you for Pauls' mother, she's amazing too. Thanks for Your guidance and counseling in my communications with my friends and colleagues and for helping me to ignore ignorant gossip and lack of understanding. Amen.

At Oakland City Train Station:

"Nice glasses," says a tall brother in all white.

"Thank you." I turn my back.

He taps me on the arm. "No, I say that because we have on the same kind." He smiles.

"I know," I answer, smiling back before I turn my back again. Instinctively, I usually don't get too friendly with folks riding the train. Not that I'm above conversing with someone occasionally. But, aside from being annoying in their small talk, one must be wary. There are just about as many deranged, strange and dangerous folk as there are kind and interesting ones. I've been living in this city long enough to understand this. And, aside from all of that, I could give less than two fucks about the fact that we're wearing the same kind of glasses!

Later:

Got through the day. Completed the important things. Intake reviews went well. Didn't get through the various lists, but that's okay. Stopped downtown at Woolworth's to get cigarettes.

Need to call my baby boy, Keith, my friend, Shirley and my writers' group peeps. Absolutely must write Ransom. His respect and love means everything to me. I'm trusting in the Most High to give him peace as well as understanding in his heart.

Don't know why this bus is sitting here. The # 83 never sits. Maybe after rush-hour, it waits around like some of the other bus's do, but I don't recall ever waiting before.

Anticipating getting some great movies this weekend. Got to decide on a book for the book club this weekend also.

Dear Father/Mother, Author of all things, keep me in mind of the abundance of the universe, that there is enough to go around for everyone. I come to You with open hands, that I may receive my share. My will is Your Will. Amen.

There's an elderly brother that just boarded the bus. He's talking to a heavily made-up sister who looks 50-ish. She has huge hips and the cellulite in her thighs and buttocks are evident because she's wearing a skin-tight pant suit made of a flimsy material, I think it's called Spandex. Her face is painted with beige make-up, orange lip-stick and lots of jet-black eye-liner and mascara. It's obvious that she's not bad-looking underneath all of the gook. Okay, so the old brother is telling the story of his story. He's speaking to her, but he speaks loud so that all can hear and she's listening attentively.

"Yeah, it was in the 70's and we had five children! I never married her. But I worked hard and provided for her. I was working two jobs. But she was laying up in the bed with someone else while I worked!"

"Did your kids tell you?" Asked the woman.

"Naw, people up and down the street would tell me. Folks was laughing at me behind my back. Talkin' bout me like a dog. This cat layin' up in my bed, over my kids while I worked!"

This old brother wore red suspenders and talked in the old-school 'hip' manner. He moved with lots of energy as he pimped through the aisle.

"Yeah, I left her. Couldn't take it. She didn't even care. Didn't miss a beat. The court ordered me to pay five hundred dollars a month! In the 70's! A hundred dollars for each child!"

"One hundred for each child!" The woman was incredulous.

"Yeah. Had to pay it too. Yeah, moved into a little one-room shack and would work and come home to this little room and eat sardines out of the can. Yeah, man, that's all I could afford! A few sisters on the bus snickered. The brother sitting next to me grinned self-consciously and shook his head.

"Found out on down the road that she'd got on Welfare," he continued. "Gettin' five hundred dollars a month from me and got on welfare! She told them I was dead---that's what I believe. We wasn't married, you know. Don't know if they checked stuff out the way they was spose to back then cause she collected money from them for a long time, a long time. Guess they didn't have things all in the computers like they do these days. One day, I called over to the house to speak to my son. 'He' answered the phone. I asked my son what's he doing answering the phone. "He lives here, dad," he tells me. Yeah, they layin' up there eatin' steaks. He layin' on my furniture, livin' with my kids, in my house---layin' in my bed with my woman and I'm eatin' sardines out of a can---workin' my black ass off and eatin' sardines out of a can in a one-room shack!"

Everyone on the bus was in stitches by this time. It was more the tone he used rather than the content of what he was saying. He was obviously enjoying the attention, like any good comedian. I couldn't help thinking he was 'profiling' his ass off as we used to say back in the day. Just talking shit. If anything, he probably was the one that this particular woman cheated 'with' instead of the victim that he proclaimed himself to be. Just no way he could tell the story with such joy and anticipation if this had actually happened to 'him.' Is it me? Man, I've seen a lot, I may be a bit jaded. Whatever.

This guy that just exited the train had two children with him. The smallest was in a baby carriage. He was being very attentive to them. Large expressive eyes with no darkness, attractive young man. He kneeled in front of the carriage and let the child pull on his gold chain. He smiled as he talked to her. Before getting off at West End, he began talking to himself... and responding in a different voice and gesturing as if someone was next to him and the child. I tried to un-see it...it was unnerving. You just never know, man.

Here we are at Oakland City Station. Who should plop down next to me but a brother full of booze. Could smell it as soon as he sat down. It's obvious the heat's gotten to him. He drops his head into his hands. God knows he couldn't feel good out here in this heat! He hasn't moved or lifted his head since he sat down. Trying to hold on.

Looks like we may get some rain.

There's a young woman on the other side of the intoxicated brother with all of her hair cut off except on the top and around the ears. What's left is platinum blond. Almost white. She's acorn brown and very thin. She's rolling her eyes at the drunken one. He raises his head for a few seconds. He couldn't take it, had to drop it back down in his hands.

Now we're boarding the #83. Hope it's not going to be a long wait. Right now I'm very hungry. Here we go, we're moving. Maybe I'll get some hot wings. A movie, maybe. Need to relax, you know, G? Get a money-order for Ransom. Postage stamps, too.

There's a chocolate-brown sister sitting directly in front of me with reddish-brown hair. It is very long and in a pony-tail. I can't tell if it's a piece or not, but it looks great. Her hair is wavy, she certainly wears it well whether it's fake or not.

Where in the world are all these people going? The crowd is absolutely unreal! This sister next to me appears to be trying to read what I'm writing. God bless you girl!

I think they've renovated most of these apartments on Campbellton Road. They look one hundred percent better. There's a lot of signs for Marvin Errington for Mayor. In yards, on corners, etc.

Later:

Made this Intake day. It wasn't easy. Had all Combo Cases except for one. The last one I was supposed to see stomped out just before I went out to the waiting room, I'm told. She threatened the front desk workers:

"I'm gonna get Channel 2 Action News to come in here and see how ya'll just sit around this front desk and bull-shit and shit," she said. "Got folks waitin' all day. This shit is for the birds. I'm gonna get all yall fired!"

The way I felt, I was glad she'd left after being told about her attitude. Tired as I was, she could've called President Clinton for all I cared. And of course, everyone knew she was waiting on me and had to make it a point of letting me know that they knew. Bitches! Sorry, G, but I'm just saying.

I'm on the Oakland City bus now. A fine young brother (and I mean 'foin,' a term used by many of us sisters for really handsome brothers) is pissed off at the driver: "Goddam, man, can't you wait?" He's with what I assume is his little boy. "Hold on a minute, Holmes, let us get on good...start this motha-fucka before somebody can get on good!" His anger appeared short-lived as he fussed with the child.

"What you want to eat, man? Want a hamburger, huh?" He could have been talking to an adult.

9/2/97

Morning, my G

I got into 'A Course in Miracles' last night. Don't know why I ever stray from it. It is such an eye-opener, a true inspiration! And it has to be among the best 'spiritual poetry' out there if there is such a thing. But above all, it steers me back on the path to truth.

Ransom called me on Saturday as expected. The Creator must have heard my prayers. He seemed fine in the sense that he's accepting things as they are.

Two young women two seats behind me are commenting about someone in their apartment complex being evicted.

"Seems like every other week somebody's getting set out, she said.

"I ain't paying no one-ninety-fo," says the other.

"Have you told your caseworker?"

"No, but I'm going to."

They're busy out here on Campbellton Road this morning. Men in hard yellow hats.

I didn't write any letters this weekend. However, we had a very productive weekend. Saturday, I paid the rent. Paul gave me money to pay the phone bill. Sent Ransom forty dollars. Later, I cleaned the bedroom meticulously as well as the bathrooms. It was contagious. The enthusiasm, I mean. Paul got out front outside and began cleaning. We discovered that the block of cement on the patio is broken off badly in the corner. There are all kinds of bugs and insects underneath it. We cleaned up the best we could, removing branches and debris and trashing it. It wasn't difficult at all working together as we did. We then repotted a plant for me. I learned a lot watching Paul as he pointed out things. This is the Paul I love. He let me put the plant into the dirt and pack it down. It was pleasurable in spite of the heat.

Evening:

Well, there's one down. Made it through the day. Didn't accomplish too much. My excuse is that it was too hot and I was sleepy. Did get a decent start on my Production Report and I phoned Georgia Power regarding the electric bill. That worked out okay. I called Paul this afternoon and he says Maintenance did show up today. The brother says he has to get a part to repair the refrigerator. Apparently, the door isn't closing entirely. Also, he put a bulb in the patio area and fixed the toilet in the downstairs guest bath. I'm so glad. I called back over to the office and spoke again to Barbara. I explained about the broken patio cement. She agreed to send someone over to look at it. Hopefully, we'll get it repaired.

Omar came over again on Sunday. He came at dinner-time as usual. He never says thanks for the meal or anything. What's up with that? A grown man? I don't really mind, I love breaking bread with others… but, well…whatever. He is Paul's cousin, but so what! No one likes to feel like they're being taken for granted. Even our grown children show their appreciation for a meal!

Tonight I'm going to eat early and get some rest. Also, guess I'd better find out where exactly the Stress-Management seminar is being held. Forgot tomorrow is Wednesday already. Got to get on it.

9/4/97
Journal Entry

Yesterday was quite Interesting. Went to the Stress-Management class. Expected boredom, but it wasn't like that at all in spite of the fact that nothing new was said. The brother who did the presentation said, "There's nothing new under the sun, but you must find a new and better way of doing and/or saying something. I appreciate that kind of honesty.

This morning, along the worksite on Campbellton Road, I'm seeing not only orange work hats but also yellow and blue. Wonder if there's any significance in that? Does this indicate a hierarchy of sorts? Oh, there's some white hats there also. Are the blue hats Foreman? Or is it the white hats? Nah, doubt it. There's too many colors out there. I'm not making light, I have high regards for what these guys do. Building things, making life a little more modern and convenient for the rest of us. And yes, I do feel that it's a man's domain. Females should not be out there breaking their nails, or worse, collecting mounds of dirt under them. Nor should they wear hard-hats and steel-toed boots. Sweating and cursing all day. That's a man's thing. Of course, that's just me, G. Some women actually like doing this kind of stuff, or they like the money, anyway. Happen to know one or two, come to think of it.

There's a nice cool breeze at Oakland City this morning. It's crowded, probably due to the lateness of the hour. Crowded on the train as well. Didn't get a seat until we reached West End Station.

9/9/97
Journal Entry

G ot out of the apartment at 8:10 this morning. Caught the #82 across from the bank right away. Looks as if I may make it on time.

Got up at 5:30, did 250 sit-ups, showered, fixed my lunch, read the Daily Word from lyanla VanZant. Paul fixed me a sandwich of turkey-bacon and boiled egg on wheat toast for breakfast. Naturally, I packed it with my lunch. I'll be eating it this morning before I begin Intake interviews.

It feels like a sauna on this train! Usually, there's some cool air, not this morning! We're scheduled to get rain today. It's all cloudy and dingy-looking out there already.

Last night, I read more of the new manual procedures. Much of it is ridiculous. Must take it in stride and do my best, of course. What else can you do? There's so much expected and so much to learn. Meanwhile, the projected number of cases each of us are supposed to have has not materialized. Most of us still have well over 150 cases! The problem is always the same. Totally unrealistic.

Later:

I haven't worked this hard in years. Got to stop staying late. Got to get a grip. Do what I can and call it a day.

I'm going into the turn-sty at Five Points a few moments ago. This young man, looks like a teenager...stops me.

"Hey, will you go over there and get me a #20 bus schedule?" He didn't even say 'please.' I didn't miss a beat. I just looked him in the eye and said, "No I won't," and let that sink in as I walked away. I didn't even look back. The nerve of him to stop me! He couldn't have been over seventeen years old. I mean, all these young sisters and brothers walking through Five Points and he stops me! I mean, it's a matter of respect, I could be his mother! Come to think of it, maybe that's why he stopped me, ha ha! But it didn't help that his damn pants were sagging off his ass! That coupled with the fact that I'm mentally and physically exhausted. It really pissed me off, man! It's crazy working this hard and being this stressed. No one appreciates it. No one. My last client today went to sleep on me. I wasn't mad at him, I didn't even care!

9/11/97
Journal Entry

I am so angry! The nerve of the #82 bus driver to be so late. Of all mornings! Because I had to stop in Kroger to get snacks for the Anti-Stress party, I decided to get the #82 out front. Wouldn't you know it would be late. Any other morning, I would've crossed the street to get one of several other buses. On top of which I could have been on time. It's always about Murphy's Law around here! Whatever can go wrong will go wrong. Unfortunate, but that's how it is. Talk to you later. We're approaching Garnett Station.

Later:

I worked quite late tonight. Thank God I didn't have to wait long for a bus. Only a few minutes. I'm exhausted but I needed to clean up some things and organize. You know how that can be, G?

A guy in front of me is reading the Bible. Bless you, brother, Lord knows we all need to be steadfast in the truth, wherever and however we can find it.

Just arrived at Oakland City Station. You wouldn't believe how loud the motor is on this bus! The driver's nowhere in sight. Hope this contraption don't need servicing. It's rattling like mad. But then, these old buses tend to do that when idling.

There's the driver now. We're taking off. The rattling was driving me bananas! Air-conditioning is up really high. Needed, I guess.

Hope I'm home for my show 'Living Single." I forget what comes on before it, the new show. I know they've taken 'Martin' off. Haven't been able to process that yet. Crazy about that show. Too bad, man.

Well, this is my flex weekend. Going to try and be productive. Writing mostly and then chilling and watching movies. Straighten up the apartment. Nothing heavy, it's not really dirty.

I'm feeling really proud of Paul today and I'm thankful to the Creator for his sobriety. It's touching to see him pulling himself together and caring about things, again. I have faith that it's all good, that his motives and intentions are pure and for both of our highest good.

I felt bad for Nita today. No one showed up for our Anti-Stress bash which was her idea. Talk about some sorry folks. Everyone in our little circle is always complaining and talking negative shit but when it comes to taking positive action to try and make things better, forget about it. Couldn't even take fifteen minutes to break a little bread and share our issues! It's crazy. And Nita acts as if nothing bothers her. I know she was hurt. Actually, I was hurt for her as well as pissed. But that's how Nita is, she never shows her emotions until they build up and then she will go off on you at some inappropriate time (the last time was at our book club meeting when everyone else was feeling festive and ready for a fun time). She didn't even speak on it, not one word, which made it even more awkward. It was weird.

9/15/97
Journal Entry

Morning, G. It's a beautiful morning. The long weekend's over. Took care of all the bills except one credit card. I phoned them and requested that they cancel it. I was informed that this transaction will be reported to the credit bureau and blah blah blah! I'll have to accept that. I'm going to document and send some correspondence to that agency also, to keep the record straight.

There's a sister sitting up front who keeps getting up and making some transaction at the pay area. She's wearing a neon-green pants-suit and long braids. She has a huge ass and her pants camouflage absolutely nothing. Why do sisters do this? Her butt shakes like jello. You can tell that in a few years her firmness will be completely gone, even though she appears very young. Don't ask me how I know this. Women just know these things.

Things didn't go exactly as planned for Paul. His intentions were to buy himself some pants with a portion of his money, but it didn't work out that way. When I left him this morning, he had his head in his hands. He mumbled that he was disgusted and didn't feel well. I tried to encourage him. "You'll get through this, dust yourself off, babe." I rubbed the back of his neck gently. "Why don't you go up and take a shower, open the blinds, let some sun in and read your gratitude list… try it." No use beating him further down, it doesn't work, I know from experience that this would just send him back out there. He has been making some progress. Right now I'm trying to focus on that.

"Okay," he said. Sounded a little stronger.

Later:

Made this Monday okay. Didn't get much work done, spent most of the day returning phone calls and responding to complaints which always wears me out. We went to lunch at Taco Macs. Service was awful. I bought Latifa's lunch in appreciation of her making greeting cards on the computer. Gail and I didn't eat anything. I had coffee and she had her Slim-fast.

We discussed my selection for next month's book-club meeting. 'The Millionaire Next Door.' Nita had already spoken to me about the selection earlier. "Several members don't like your selection and don't want to read the book, June. Would you be willing to make a change?"

"No," I said. "We can discuss it at lunch."

At lunch, Cindy said she'd taken a look inside the book and all she saw was a lot of charts. Gail went 'Ugh! I don't think so, June."

"I wasn't exactly thrilled with some of the books that you guys selected in the past, but I got through them," I said. I held my ground. "Remember when we started this club? We said that our goal was to read different types of books and expand our minds. Does anyone remember that?"

"Yeah, yeah," someone mumbled. We left it at that. The remainder of lunch was spent complaining and laughing at the waitresses. Yet it was no joke because the service was very shabby. Nita volunteered to formally complain to management resulting in us not having to pay the bill. We all liked that and agreed to leave a nice tip for our server. We made it back to the office a few minutes after 2:00 pm, which was good.

Later in the afternoon, I decided to change the book selection. I want it to be something everyone is willing to read and discuss. I decided not to take it that serious. We also discussed going to the Million Woman March on Oct 25th. We're going to rent a van.

9/10/97
Journal Entry

Thank God for Paul. In spite of our issues, he's always been able to help me put things in the proper perspective (when he's clean and in his right mind). I've got to call him and tell him that when I reach work. We talked last night.

"Read that stuff at work. If I were you I'd sit at my desk with that manual open and read it when necessary. That's part of your job isn't it?" Of course this is easy for him to say, he has an MBA in business and used to be a bank officer in New York and I'm just a lowly case manager working for the state of Georgia, an entirely different culture. However, he's right. There's no real reason for me to bring manuals home. The work isn't going to change, it's always going to be too much. This fact alone causes me stress. Let me place this in the Creator's hands. Amen.

There must be a fire back there at Cascade Pines. I've seen two fire trucks streaking past the bus this morning. One of them turned into Cascade Pines.

Here are the hard-hats again. They're busy in front of S&S Cafeteria and Campbellton Plaza.

9/16/97
Journal Entry

I did three hundred crunches this morning. Showered, made coffee and left the apartment at 8:20. I had thought about taking today off as a Holy Day according to Louis Farrakhan who decreed today a Holy Day of Atonement for black people. However, due to the volume of work I have pending, decided against it. Additionally, Wednesday, I've got training and next week I've got three days of training! It's going to be difficult, as it is, to complete all of my work for this month.

I was fortunate to catch the #83 bus as soon as I got some cash and bought cigarettes at the BP on the corner. I feel great this morning.

Yesterday, I took the time to write Ransom. Instead of sending him a money order in an envelope (his words), I enclosed a letter also. Felt good about that. After all, if I write no one else, I should write him. Sure he will appreciate it.

I've got to get some work done today. Goofed off, or shall I say, did my own thing for most of the day yesterday. I did take the time to read new policy. However, God knows, I don't have a clue what it's about. Very few of us do, it's crazy. Actually, it's not a matter of understanding it, it's that the sheer volume of changes is over-whelming and it's incredulous that we're expected to implement all of this stuff ASAP!

Later:

Accomplished quite a bit today. Completed most of my new cases. Got organized and straightened the office. Left some directions for Barbara to do while I'm off tomorrow, or rather, while I'm in training.

There's this sister behind me on the phone talking to her child, obviously. She's actually yelling. Then there's these little children, one next to me and the other two across from me.

Their mother is begging them to sit down and be quiet to no avail. They're busy jumping all over the seats and screaming. Thank goodness, we're approaching Oakland City station. There's the #83 bus arriving now, too. Oops! That was the #80 Allison Court.

Hope Paul's in a better mood. He appeared some better yesterday evening and this morning, but then he became stressed dealing with Social Security on the phone. He called and relayed this to me earlier this afternoon.

Where's that #83 anyway? It's cooling off some, thank goodness. Here's the #83. Huh, oh, she's screaming and yelling at another bus driver. We've just boarded now we have to get off and get another bus. Someone shouted, "We just want to get home, lady!"

There's another sister cracking her gum directly in my ear as I write! What an idiot! And I'm telling you, these are the loudest buses! All this shaking and rumbling, the loud air-conditioner and motor and the voices…the incessant non-stop thunderous chatter! Geez, I've had it. Sometimes it seems intolerable!

9/17/97
Journal Entry

Training:

Boring, boring, boring bull! I'm going to make the most of this. It is insulting but maybe we can get something from this. What, you ask? I don't know but we'll see! The insulting part is how they bend over backwards attempting to make it sound like this is all going to be a smooth transition when we all know it's going to be chaos. Hell, a normal day is chaos at DFACS…a little honesty would be so much more respectful.

"Model Work"

"Not Yet"

Dry cleaners that have clothes left over can donate these clothes for our "Dress for Success" program.

Flex-time people-We're going to be working non-traditional hours.

AHA Housing Contract (24 months working get the difference of rent back, like a savings account)

Northwest Office-Job Centers-Computers for clients to access Dept. of Labor (DOL) and Bulletin Board.

Dept. of Family and Children Services (DFACS) DeKalb County-Job Fare every Monday (must wear Business Suit)

9/19/97
Journal Entry

Today promises to be a day of first. I'm on Intake today and I'm going to try something new. My goal is to be innovative and creative. I did do a group interview of sorts last week with my on-going clients. Today I will try it with my new people. To the extent that I can anyway. Also, we're going to be on the radio this evening! Don Roundtree, an Atlanta poet, called Paula, the white sister in my writers' group, invited our entire group to read. I'm thrilled! He says that three other people cancelled. Good for us. Wonder if Gwen Brown's going to be there. I kind of miss her. She's been such an inspiration. If she doesn't come, I'm going to touch basis with her in the near future.

Hope no one wants this seat. It's getting crowded in here. Know that's selfish but hey, it's hot. But I will give it up. There, just did, for an elderly man, thank you very much.

Yesterday, a teenager killed another teenager in DeKalb County. Another senseless killing! There is no understanding about this. No justification. The children of that school are being offered counseling today. It's mind-boggling. The drugs and the killings are destroying our communities. Parents are burying their children. This disturbs me the most. Burying a child…anybody's child. Where is the hope? Our black leaders need to have a conversation in the street and on the corners with our own…about this situation. We need to deal with this. It's warfare out here on these streets, a state of emergency! I certainly don't have any answers but I pray that God—the Most High, will send someone…

9/20/97
Journal Entry

Morning, G Man, I get so frustrated with these idiots in Atlanta, with all their petty rules and regulations. They can come up with a million and one ways to humiliate and degrade you! Honestly! I left home this morning short thirty-five cents of my train fare. Yeah, I know that sounds pathetic. Okay, so I went to Krogers, down the street from me, to withdraw a few dollars from my checking account. Wouldn't you know it, my Tillie Card would not access my account! "Sorry, cannot help you," it said. Of course, I was pissed. I knew I only had twenty dollars or so in my account, so I decided to buy something and debit the amount from my account. Naturally, I chose cigarettes. Okay, the cashier, a heavy white sister whose attitude I never liked, didn't even bother to ask if I wanted change back when she rang up the cigarettes.

I say to her, "You didn't ask me if I wanted cash back?" She goes, "Sorry Mam, we can't do that before 8:00 am." I just looked at her. I never could think fast on my feet when I get frustrated. I didn't think to ask her to take back one of the packs of cigarettes. I just stomped away, irritated. Then I got the brilliant idea to take one pack to the BP gas station next door to get an exchange. Of course this young sister gave me an argument. "Mam, I can't accept those cigarettes. Did you get them from here?"

"Yes I lied

"Well, mam, we have a policy and our inventory has to come out right, I don't know if you bought them from here or not and you're not showing me a receipt."

"What difference does it make whether I got them from here or not? I mean really! You're going to sell them, regardless, aren't you? I mean sista to sista, give me a break! I was incredulous, especially with the look she gave me!

"Mam, that's our policy, I'm sorry." She turned away, dismissing me. I was livid. Get me the manager," I shouted.

"Mam, I am the manager." She couldn't have been a day over twenty. I left. Finally, it dawned on me that if I was going to exchange the cigarettes, I may as well go back to Kroger's! With dread, I trudged on back over to Kroger's. Naturally, there was a line of folks and only one line open. A few minutes after I got in line, a young sister opened up another line, only to inform me that she could not give me cash. I would have to go to the Customer Service Center, she said. It would open up at 8:00 am and it was 8:00 am now.

"Okay, but as you can see, they haven't opened yet. Come on, I've got to get to work!" I said. She seemed to consider, then she picked up the phone and called the person who was in charge of CS, probably the heavy, light-skinned woman who's always back there. She listened and then repeated the same garbage to me again about waiting. Finally, I gave up and purchased a bar of candy and asked for ten dollars in cash by using my Tillie Card again. It was really a frustrating morning. In retrospect, it's laughable, but not so funny at the time. Like they say, if you're broke, you're a joke in this city and right now, I am a serious joke. Ha ha!

Got a little done today. Several reviews, four... and then I was able to place several clients in employment activities. That was a biggy.

On my way home, it's Friday and I'm thankful. Didn't work too hard today. Let's see what the weekend brings.

9/22/97
Journal Entry

Man, I don't know what my problem was this weekend. The radio station was interesting. Wasn't as nervous as I thought I would be. Hal allowed us to read several poems each. Harold and I left before 8:30 pm. We both had read most of what we had with us. When I got home I called Monica. She sounded terrible. I guess the strain of her sisters' illness and running back and forth to the hospital has gotten to her. I wished her well and asked her to call me later in the week. Then I called some of the other writers to remind them of our Saturday meeting at Colony Square. As it turned out, none of them showed. But Shane put in an appearance. He brought his mother along. She's visiting from L.A. The meeting was actually good, but I've gone over all that already.

The problem was with me physically and mentally. And, well, emotionally too. I felt down, irritable and tired. Maybe it was simply fatigue. It shows up in many forms. My mind seemed to shut down Friday at one point, while I was calling the other writers. I was trying to tell Kelly's significant other where our meeting was being held and my mind just went blank. If he hadn't had a sense of humor, I would've felt humiliated. I did call back a little later, however. That was kind of scary. Then Saturday, after I returned home as well as Sunday afternoon, I couldn't write a single thing. Not one single word. It was downright unsettling. I not only felt exhausted but discouraged. Anyway, finally, last night I opened up 'A Course in Miracles' and began reading. It's what I needed to help me to get back on track and focus.

9/23/97
Journal Entry

On my way to Training. Out here rolling on the westbound train to the Northwest Office. I'm in no mood for any nonsense from these people this morning. I left that questionnaire at work yesterday. Didn't complete it anyway and I needed to complete it at home. Didn't have time to do it at the office. Forget it. I would have loved to be on time this morning, but exercising and preparing my lunch is important too. Listen, there I go, G! On my pitty-pot.

I wonder if my left arm is bothering me because I write all the time. Hope that's the reason and nothing else. Also, hope I don't miss this bus that'll get me to the Northwest office on time. Well, it's going to be three days of a lot of information. Information over-load as far as I'm concerned. Please help me to deal with this stuff and see things in a more positive light. Thanks. It's already done.

9/24/97
Journal Entry

S econd day of Employment Services Training. I think I may have forgotten who I am temporarily. All the job changes, the training and being behind is the only thing I can think about. I find it so hard to accept and yet there's no getting around it, got to go through it. With God's Grace this will all fall into place somehow.

Left my umbrella there yesterday. Hope it's still there because we're threatened with rain for the rest of the week. The rain itself is fine with me. It calms me.

Went to Five Points yesterday to see if my book "A Course in Miracles' was at the Lost and Found. I know I left it on the train when I exited there. The young sister there said normally it takes a couple of days and advised me to check back today. I informed her politely that I'd tried to reach her office repeatedly for two days straight without reaching anyone. She went through a routine about lunch hour being between one and two o'clock. I have to agree with Mr. Pride, my colleague and partner in crime, customer service in general has gone to hell. The sister at Five Points didn't even pretend to care about my situation. The problem is lack of pride in what you do, even if you're not making a lot of money. You'd stand a better chance of being promoted or getting a better paying position if you put your best foot forward. It's truly frustrating transacting any business in this city and I'm not the only one complaining. To be treated with respect and courtesy is the exception rather than the norm here. I'm talking about my people. Black people. No, then again, whites also. Many of them withhold information or act as if they don't know. Later, you realize that this is done on purpose. Nasty and rude constantly. Lack of professionalism is an understatement! Lately, I found myself taking the time to commend the folks who are kind and helpful without an attitude. I've even gone to their managers and put in a good word on their behalf to show my appreciation. But it's a shame, this should be the norm.

Later:

What a day! I can't believe what the State wants us to do. Because of President Clinton, the Feds have started new programs, but I'd bet money it's not this difficult anywhere as it is in the state of Georgia! Specifically, the way it's being administered. Why didn't they make some credible plans before these Work Plans were put into place? Turns out, we've completed these mass group reviews and even some one-on-one reviews on every one of our clients, which is in the thousands, only to learn that every one of them are wrong! Every last one of them have got to be done over! I've been at this game long enough not to expect anything to make sense, but this is beyond the pale. A bunch of bullshit! I've got to continue until I get a better position, going to make it my business to apply for something else. I'm thinking Quality Assurance or Medicaid. There's rarely positions available in these departments, though. Nobody leaves once they get there, the pay is good, rarely do they see clients and they don't work like slaves. I really haven't applied myself the way that I should, got to get on it. It's like playing the lottery, you've got to play to win.

Last night, I drank three glasses of ice-tea (I love the stuff) to kill my thirst, I must have eaten a lot of salt yesterday. Anyway, I knew I wouldn't be able to get to sleep after all that caffeine so I took one of Paul's sleeping pills. That pill really worked. Paul tried to give me two, but something told me to only take one. A good thing, too. I began to feel the effects about a half an hour after I'd taken it. I actually drank another half glass of tea and still went to sleep.

9/25/97
Journal Entry

T hank goodness, this is the last day of training. My hope is that we are released early. Since it's raining and everyone's got to be sick to death of these Work Plans, I'm confident we will. I need to get to the bank before they close and do some food shopping.

Wow, I'm bored to tears, others are busy completing mock Work Plans. God bless them. I simply refuse, can't really learn that way. Sorry. Peering around the room, I can see that I'm not the only one. I see Gary and Delores over there not even pretending to participate. They both slept all of Tuesday and most of today. Hilarious!

Gary was telling me about the picnic they're planning for the agency for October 17, something we do every year. The committee's having a taste test this week. The tentative menu is barbecued chicken, turkey burgers, hot dogs, pasta salad, potato salad, coleslaw, peach and apple cobbler, ice cream, etc., all good.

My long weekend's coming up. Plan to mostly rest, straighten up a bit and enjoy some alone time. When are we getting the hell out of here? I'm starving, need breakfast. When is break time, what is wrong with these people, it's after ten-thirty!

9/29/97
Journal Entry

I t's back to the office today, haven't been there since last Monday due to all this training. It's going to be interesting to see if I can complete the stuff I have pending. Tomorrow is the last day of the month. Geez!

Had a lovely weekend in spite of all the rain. I love the rain. Much of my time was spent in my king-sized bed. Mentally, I was exhausted by the end of the week and it kind of came down on me. Paul and I played one match of Scrabble each morning on Friday and Saturday, we skipped Sunday because I remained in bed until noon. By the time I got up and made a quick run to Kroger's to pick up tomato sauce and celery for Spaghetti, Paul's cousin, Omar, was there. They played Chess while I cooked. After we ate (the spaghetti was delicious) I called my friend, Melissa. She's a white sister that I met at one of Paul's NA meetings. Her husband's in recovery as well and we sort of bonded. She's hilarious, acts like she's black, which is pretty common when you're married to a black man. Anyway, I got her on board to come over and give me a hand during my book-club meeting. She's considering joining so this would be good for her to check us out. I'm not sure what I'm going to serve yet but it's important to me not to blow my budget.

Someone nearby on this bus smells great! I've smelled it before but don't know what it is.

It seems as though I'm blocked, paralyzed or something. Mentally worn. Hopefully it's only temporary. I need to get something completed, submit something somewhere. I've got to organize my writing, got so much incomplete stuff, but the thought of doing it overwhelms me. I place myself up there on the bed amid all my stuff and do everything except that. I read, listen to jazz… I'm rambling. There's no need to… well…just need to get it done.

Later:

Made this Monday. Got work galore. I put a dent in it, but there's so much more to do. Nita got on my nerves today. Using my computer printer while I'm trying to use it. What's up with that? Why can't people give you your props without you having to check them? Oh well. I don't know why I worry about hurting Nita's feelings, she's the type that will check you in a 'New York' minute, yet she's very sensitive when the shoe is on the other foot. But I feel like she asked for it today, she takes too much for granted.

The # 83 isn't here yet. Surprising. There, okay, we just boarded the #83. Man is it crowded! And I really dislike this new seating they have. You sit directly facing people and you almost have to make eye contact. You can see the discomfort in most faces.

Be glad when tomorrow's over. I'm going to put in for a Medicaid position which is open at the CNN office. I'm sure it will be less work as well as less stress in this department. Also, the next time a Quality Assurance position is open, I'm not going to hesitate to apply for it. I saw Cliff today, he used to be in my Unit but now he's a Fraud Investigator. He says when I put in for a QA position to let him know. He'll put in a good word for me. He knows a few 'higher ups' there. I certainly will. Cliff is cool. He tends bar on the side at an upscale club in Midtown and hires himself out on weekends for special occasions and parties for friends. He did a couple of gigs for me when I hosted friends and family when they came into town. His fees are very reasonable plus he has a great personality. People always remember him and ask about him. I can see why he does well.

Sometimes the #83 seems like the longest ride in the world. Slowest driver all the time. Guess I'm just tired. Almost home, thank goodness.

9/30/97
Journal Entry

All thanks, love and appreciation to the Magnificent, glorious Creator! There is much to be thankful for. I always lack faith, never feeling that I have as much as I should. I feel foolish when I think about it because I know that You move mountains for those who have faith and try to be righteous. Thank You for everything.

Slept well last night. Woke up to the delicious aroma of Pauls' salmon, grits and coffee. He's a 'Right Reverend' in a few areas, this is one of them. And he was in good spirits, not overly anxious, which is rare for him, you know. We got out of the house at 6:35 am because he had a VA appointment at 8:30. We went to Kroger's to get money from the ATM. He asked to borrow twenty dollars until tomorrow. That's all! I didn't have a problem with that.

There was no evidence of a raise on this pay. Not going to panic. It's probably scheduled for the pay in the middle of the month. That's right, this isn't even October yet. This is Septembers' pay. I can smell the cigarette in my pocket. That's okay, I'm an addict. Anyway, I'm on the #83 headed for work and it's only 7:10, which is good because this is the last day of the month and I've got plenty of work to complete today.

Paul was talking to Keith about getting back in school. "If he's going to get his Masters, he needs to get back in there now, he'll be twenty-eight years old before you know it. Matter of fact, if he goes back now, he'll be twenty-eight by the time he gets it. You don't want to wait much longer than that, you know. Cause it's going to take him three years anyway."

"Yeah, I said. "That's why I want you to go down there with me for Thanksgiving. I know he wants you to see what he's accomplished. He wants to have that kind of dialogue with you. Wants you to see that he's a man now. It would be good if you could make it, Paul."

He continued on about the importance of Keith getting back in school without acknowledging what I said. But I knew he heard me. I listened to him. What he said made plenty of sense, too.

Later:

This workday is over, thank goodness. Paul is home. Can't believe it! Says he made it to VA this morning. He's upbeat, watching the game. Good, I didn't ask any questions. Sometimes it's just about peace.

10/1/97
Journal Entry

I was completely exhausted when I got off yesterday. Didn't even bother to write anything while on the train. I'd called ahead and checked to see if Paul wanted something. He wanted a burger. I got off of the bus at the back of Greenbriar Mall, near home and bought myself some Rib-tips (something I didn't need) and a cheeseburger and fries for Paul. When I got home, Paul walked up to the front of our complex and bought cokes out of the machine. I only ate half the tips. The rest I'm taking for today's lunch. Paul said he's going to pay Malcolm what he owes him today. I asked him to leave me a hundred dollars. Besides the main bills, I've got to get vitamins, eye-care products and a money order for Ransom. Feeling grateful for this budget I created for myself.

Later:

I'm off. Today went pretty well.

I tell you this train conductor has it going on! He sounds like a TV announcer, very articulate and deliberate. It's almost absurd. Usually when he's on, passengers laugh and make comments, positive comments. No one laughed or commented today. Guess they're getting used to him.

10/2/97
Journal Entry

I have mixed emotions about today. Got a late start for one thing. Being late on my own time is one thing, but holding someone else up is something different. As I dashed around the corner of the IBEW building, Tracy and Brenda, who work in my unit...pulled up beside me. They were just pulling off to make it to the meeting at the OIC building. I jumped in the back seat.

"Sorry I'm late, I said. Just knew I had missed you guys. I couldn't get it together this morning. Can't believe I caught you!"

Tracy laughed in that squeaky voice of hers. "Girl, I just got here five minutes ago. You know I'm late every day. I thought I'd be holding you and Brenda up. Here you hadn't even gotten here yet!" We arrived at the OIC in plenty of time. Staff was still milling around looking for coffee and coke. Tracy and I followed Brenda down to the front area of the auditorium.

"I don't know why in the world we let Brenda lead us all the way down to the front," Tracy squeaked. I didn't really mind, but I sat down and promptly dozed off. The next thing I knew, I heard Brenda and Tracy snickering. Right then, I knew my own snoring had awakened me, I had to laugh at myself. There was a female speaker from DOL on the podium going on and on and on in a monotone drone. As I looked around the room, it was apparent that she had put a lot of others to sleep. It was really painful. We thought we'd only get an over-view of DOL'S partnership with DFAC's, but this sister got deep into various details. Anyway, the remaining speakers, Marie Young, a guy from PIC and another DOL administrator (who was very lively) must have been just as bored as the rest of us because they were careful to keep their presentations to a minimum. Herbert Johnson was among them, but, being a man of few words, he took this opportunity not to say anything at all. But the male DOL administrator made it known that Herbert was responsible for most of the new program. I think many were amazed to hear this. The general perception about Herbert is that he functions at a minimum and draws a large pay check and doesn't really give a damn, period. I, however, don't happen to agree as I've observed him closely and found him to be quite good at what he does, but he has this laid-back, slow demeanor which is deceptive. I respect the brother because he is very fair in his treatment of staff. On one occasion, not long ago, I had to have a conference with him regarding a complaint leveled against me by a Quality Assurance Supervisor who really had it in for me (we've bumped heads a couple of times before in the past). As I sat there in his office and presented my side of the story, he appeared to be asleep lounging in his chair with his eyes down-cast. But when I'd finished, he slowly and methodically repeated a summary of everything I'd said and even gave me some good advice. Later, I found out that he'd ruled in my favor, so there. He's alright with me. People around the office don't always know what they're talking about. Peace, here's my stop. Later.

10/3/97

G ood Morning, G!
All thanks to the Creator who strengthens me and through whom I have all power. Thanks to you as well for being my Guardian Angel, G. I know I take you for granted and don't always stay on course, but then that's why you're assigned to me, right! Sorry, G…that's disrespectful. Honestly, I scare myself when I do that! Forgive me.

The wonderful Lima beans that I prepared last night have made me sick. For one thing, I ate them too late at night. I had hoped that the ginger-ale would over-ride any gastronomical problems. Boy, was I wrong!

I haven't seen or heard from Paul since Wednesday morning. Apparently, he's on one of his binges. I trust that the Creator is looking out for him. He's not my concern right now. Maybe he has an angel looking out for him, too. Maybe everyone does.

I got up this morning not caring whether I would be on time or not. Again, the beans.

Someone took my sunglasses at the meeting at OIC yesterday. I was absent-minded enough to leave them in the bathroom. Naturally, when I went back, the glasses were gone.

I guess it will be after nine by the time I get to work. I'll just turn in a leave slip. I'm just glad it's Friday. I'm supposed to write something about relationships for our writers' group assignment for Saturday. I haven't given it any thought whatsoever. Haven't had the time. However, the piece I write will be about positive male-female relationships. I get so weary of male-bashing in spite of my own personal life.

10/6/97
Journal Entry

Man, I really got a late start this morning. Just couldn't get out of bed. Got to get some vitamins as well as rest. I hate going in late when I'm on Intake, more importantly, after Mandy arrives. She's pretty understanding but I don't like having to account for myself like that. I should write an article on being late, after all, I'm an expert at it.

It's really sad that we, as a people, always have to be looking at everything in terms of race. Just pick up the newspaper. All you read about on a national level is race, race, race and more race!

The guy in front of me just yelled to the bus driver, "Come on, let's go, man. Drive, I'm already late, shit!" Those were my sentiments exactly.

I feel pretty good about the weekend. Not only did I change my bedroom around, I organized my poetry and placed it into file folders. Love my poems, need to submit them somewhere.

10/8/97
Journal Entry

G ood evening. It was another hectic day for me but I did manage to finish re-opening the Food Stamp closures. That's a BIGGIE!

This afternoon, someone claimed that three eye-witness's overheard Shelly Kellerman call a client a nigger!

10/9/97
Journal Entry

I couldn't go on yesterday. Anyway, as I was saying, several clients claimed they witnessed Shelly calling a male client a nigger. Supposedly, she called him a fat ass and lowered her voice when she said the N word. Now I really have to stretch my imagination to believe that this happened, even on a stressful day. Not saying it didn't happen, but it's hard to imagine her losing control like that. She's always been professional (she's white, by the way) and she's known to be kind and compassionate. Had she spoken directly to the man, or was she in fact talking to another worker about this person? Either way, it doesn't sound right. I want to know what happened. Wonder if any of the other staff saw what happened.

I felt really tired this morning, feels like the beginning of a head cold. Went to bed at 8:30 last night and went straight to sleep. I awoke when the alarm went off at 5:30 this morning but didn't get up immediately. I lay there somewhere in the twilight zone until Paul turned on that damn hall-way light! He knows that always works. Made coffee and sat downstairs for ten or fifteen minutes. Then I went upstairs with my coffee and sat another five minutes or so before I could actually get up and shower.

They're still working on the street on Campbellton Road. Seems to take forever to get through there. Besides that, it's very humid. We're finally at Oakland City station and the train is already here. Should get to work by eight-thirty. I'm so grateful to be off for the next four days. Going to try and be positive, productive and fun. Get some writing done.

10/21/97
Journal Entry

B een awhile. Got off track a little. Not only with this journal, with my budget as well. Spent more than I needed to on the dinner for the book club meeting. You know how it is. Easy to go over-board. Now I've got to spend more for this diet I want to go on with Gail. It's the old Grapefruit Diet supposedly from the Mayo Clinic. I'm going to try it. Don't have anything to lose except maybe a few pounds. I'm sure it's the same one I tried when I lived in Ohio years ago. Got to get stuff like grapefruit, bacon, coffee, tomatoes, honey, things I really need anyway. No need to worry about my savings. My goal was two hundred dollars a month. Looks as if it's going to be more like one hundred. Guess I should feel good about that. In the past, I haven't saved jack!

I missed the radio show on Friday and the writers' group meeting on Saturday (we named our group, the Urban Class Writers, which I think is pretty cool and aptly describe us). I really wanted to make the writers' group meeting. I'd hate to miss out on plans for anything important that may arise, especially poetry readings at coffee shops, etc. I've fallen in love with our little group. There's Harold, a Morehouse Man (he graduated from Morehouse College) who writes Science Fiction. He has a slew of stories but has never submitted anything for publication for some reason. I think he's quite good. Then there's Nicole, she's a professional chef from North Carolina. She's currently working on an autobiography of her child-hood…a very sad story. Then there's Paula, a white sister with some serious health issues. She's one of the most 'open' persons that I've ever met, very enlightened and spiritual and it shows in her poetry. She and her husband are struggling to maintain their duplex on the Eastside where there is a lot of 'gentrification' going on. She's very angry about it. They've had their property for many years…they were among the few whites that stayed on when the initial white-flight took hold in that area. Now that the new young Yuppies are moving in, they can no longer afford to stay. Then there's me. There's two others, a younger sister and a white brother, who really aren't considered part of our group because they never show up for meetings. I need to call Paula or Harold, maybe both of them, find out what's going on. I can still prepare something to send Gwen Brown before November1st.

10/22/97
Journal Entry

I finally understand that I am full of cold, hence, the headachy, tired feeling. Still, I drug myself out of bed and exercised for about thirty minutes and prepared food for the diet which I'm starting today. I did what I had to do.

I don't plan to call any of the writers before tomorrow when my weekend begins. Maybe I'll have more energy by then.

Today, we'll be sitting in another conference all afternoon. A session on family violence. Great fun (groan). It begins at one o'clock and last thru four-thirty. At least it's at the office. No extra traveling involved.

10/23/97
Journal Entry

Made it. Time for the weekend. There are some crazy people at Five Points. Hustling anything and everything you can think of! Crazy on the train too. People staring you down. Just staring. Don't know what to make of it.

Brown, white, beige, black, orange and yellow people. Wonderful, serious, studious, important, unimportant and interesting people. Fun, angry, impatient and pesky people. Don't push, brother!

It's almost dark. Probably won't reach home before seven.

Hope Paul is feeling okay. It's nearing the holidays… his time of the year to nut-up but I also know that he's overcome, to some degree, maybe he can get through.

Someone in the back of the train is playing their box much louder than usual. Whatever makes them think someone else wants to listen to their rap nonsense! Seriously, play me something to heighten my consciousness, but make me want to hear it, add some positivity, give me some pleasure, give me some hope, man! Where are all the everyday people? Where did they go? Were they an illusion?

10/28/97
Journal Entry

It's the end of the month and I've got second appointments for this morning. However, I'm more concerned with getting my poem together and getting it mailed today. I've got to get Mildred to give me a half hour, at least. Promised her I'd pay her. Gwen has to have it by Saturday.

I'm on the # 83 headed for work. It's thirty-five degrees this morning, but it feels wonderful to me. I've got my office sweater and my wool jacket on along with my basic black slacks. Also, I put on panty-hose and socks, so I'm comfortable.

We've been asked to work over-time on Saturday. They're saying just for two Saturdays but trust me, this can go on for months. It's always that way with over-time as far as the state is concerned.

Just missed the north-bound train. This is still rush –hour, should be another one shortly.

10/30/97
Journal Entry

Read some disturbing stuff last night in New Age about prayer and thought. It concerned a person's ability to do or cause harm to another through negative prayer and intent. This certainly isn't new but it's been considered to be superstitious and mythological (or so I thought). Now, these people with two and three letters behind their names are seriously discussing this stuff. I learned that most religions believe that this negative power exist. There is a way of combating these prayers through meditation, prayers, spiritual guides, etc. You can overcome. You must be conscious and aware of negative vibes, however. I'm not pretending that I really understand this. There is so much that none of us understand. I think the most disturbing thing for me was this woman's personal account of her experiences with her father. He exhibited the ability to heal as well as cause destruction, apparently through curses and negative prayer. She was really convincing in her description of the havoc that he seemingly caused. She was apparently very frightened of him and felt him to be evil incarnate. Enough of that!

As far as this diet is concerned, I'm losing some weight. Still can't really fasten some of the clothes I'm trying to get back into, but I can tell I'm losing. Even the blouse I'm wearing right now, isn't as tight as it used to be.

Evening

Finally, this work day is over. Got a lot done. Completed all of my TANF, FS and Over-payment cases. Tomorrow I just have to complete Specials, go over a TANF case, send out December appointments and complete less important miscellaneous stuff.

It was really a beautiful day. I took deep gulps of the crisp fresh air. The sun was brilliant, enhancing everything with vibrant color! Don't know why this always surprises me.

They've done a lot of work on the corner of Stanton and Campbellton Road. That little plaza has been remodeled. There's a Papa John's Pizza, another new restaurant, a new gas station and convenience store and all the trash has been cleaned up. Great.

I can smell the liquor on this guy that's sitting in front of me. He keeps belching and gulping loudly, hope he doesn't throw-up, geez!

I spend a lot of time thinking some people are strange, but what about me? Maybe I'm strange to some. Maybe be wise to look at it that way whether it's true or not. Simplifies things.

10/31/97
Journal Entry

It's Halloween, the last day of the month and the weekend. I was going to rent movies tonight, but instead I'm going to clean, make some calls and relax. Tomorrow, after Paul gives me some money, I'll see what I can do. After all, I've got to update my budget, send Ransom something, etc.

They've widened Campbellton Road where they've been working for months, but of course, they're not finished. But at least traffic can move a little faster, much of the gravel has been removed. Feels like I'm going to have a good day. If I pace myself, I should be able to complete what I need to do effortlessly.

Temperature is in the upper sixty's. We're supposed to get rain for the weekend.

Diet's coming along fine, I'm eating less in the evenings and feeling more energetic. Food does make you tired, I find. Even good food.

11/3/97
Journal Entry

I t's Monday morning. Paul's VA check didn't come, my paycheck was short due to an old check I wrote back in May which was cashed Friday by the bastards. Sorry, that's how I feel about them. Paul's worried, so am I, we really do need a boost. I'm trying to stay positive. Right now, we've got to get the rent paid.

Gail, Linda and I agreed to do group interviews this morning. I'm going in there in a positive state. We'll do okay.

We're approaching Oakland City Station now. My stomach's a little queasy, hope a cup of coffee will get me to where I need to be.

There's a guy with a baby in his arms in a small basinet. He looks comfortable enough. I assume the woman standing conversing with him is the child's mother. One never knows.

Later:

I'm off. We did pretty well with the group interviews. Fifteen of my TANF's showed and ten FS only cases. Each of us pitched in and helped the clients complete the forms and made sure everything was signed properly. After that, this afternoon, we mailed out second appointments.

I've been trying to get Paul on the phone all day with no results. I'm trying real hard to remain calm. The worse thing would be having to pay the rent late. No, worse than that would be getting a warrant and having to pay three hundred dollars in warrant fees.

The temperature's dropping. It's supposed to get down to the thirty's tonight. It's already cooler than it was this morning. But rain was in the forecast, we haven't gotten any yet. It's almost completely dark out now. It could be nine or ten o'clock pm, but it's only six-fifteen right now. I'm sleepy.

11/4/97
Journal Entry

You know me, G. You know how it is. You've been right by my side. I sense your presence often…that is, when I'm in my right mind… or in a peaceful state, whatever that is. Sometimes, I wish you would just slap me or do something to frighten me or something to keep me together. But I know it's not set up that way.

Today is Election Day. I'm not voting for anyone. Actually, I feel ashamed, this is not who I am. I work for the state, for God's sake!

Paul called me this morning. He's at Grady Memorial hospital. Thank God he's okay…well, at least he's alive. He says he called them from the streets and flagged down one of Atlanta's finest to take him there. This is not new, but he hasn't been in this state in a while. Frightened and paranoid. I can't be more thankful to hear from him, though. I need to talk to my mother!

11/5/97
Journal Entry

My stomach's aching something terrible. It may be cold. Feels as if I've been drinking alcohol or maybe some kind of food poisoning. I don't know, I'm always diagnosing myself. My primary-care Doctor is always cautioning me about that. Oh well, it's probably just stress, which is no small thing.

After leaving the dentist office yesterday, I paid the phone bill and went to Kroger and bought grapefruit juice, bacon, soda and chicken wings. I'm resuming my diet today. I didn't buy tomatoes figuring Paul will get some this week when we grocery shop. I can eat the carrots I bought the other day. I also got broccoli. Forgot to get eggs, there's only two left in the frig.

Gail agreed to see the remainder of my Intakes when I left yesterday and I'm seeing her Intakes today while she takes off. I don't mind, but when I agreed, I wasn't thinking about my monthly report which is due by noon today. Goodness! Talk about stress, that darn report usually takes all day to complete! I'll do what I can.

11/18/97
Journal Entry

I can't believe it's the middle of the month already! Christmas is upon us and the year is nearly over. I hope I can look back over this year and see some progress.

Yesterday, I came home, made coffee and sat down determined to get on with my short story. I'm discouraged with it, however. I'm not satisfied with the female character at all. I'm not sure I understand her and I don't have much empathy for her. Subsequently, I thought about presenting the story from the male point of view but I'm really not feeling him either. Maybe I should abandon the story all together. After all, I could take some of the good stuff (and I do feel there's some good stuff) and use it in an entirely new story.

It's a beautiful morning in spite of the cold. Good weather to breathe in.

Gail said yesterday that Mandy would be in an administrators meeting at the CNN office this morning. I hope she knows what she's talking about because I'm not going to reach the office before nine o'clock this morning. Not a big deal, Mandy's so cool, but I don't like taking that for granted.

11/20/97
Journal Entry

It's going to be nice today. The sun's already out, imitating spring and the temperature's mild. On Tuesday, the weatherman predicted it would be in the sixty's today. Good fresh air!

This is my last working day of the week and it's a good thing too, because I'm out of cash. It's weird that it takes a certain amount of money just to go to work.

I've dropped a few pounds, but what a price I paid! That grapefruit did a job on my stomach, even though I love it. I meditated about it, I have no need of sickness, so I'm claiming it gone already. Must take care of my health.

Paula called me last night. She had good things to say about the Urban Poetry readings. She says Nicki also read. Wish I could have been there. I told her how discouraged I am with my stories. She told me to bring one to our next meeting. She wants to meet next Saturday. I think it's time to admit to the group how thin-skinned I am. I felt some kind of way that my poem wasn't selected. I'm not proud of this feeling at all. Wonder how the others felt. Speaking of which, I need to call Betty. Also, Paula is a pretty good poet in my opinion. So to myself I say 'get over it."

This weekend I'm playing some of my motivational tapes, specifically, Wayne Dyer and Iyanla Vanzant. These two gurus never fail to lift me higher. I will be writing my goals for 1998 and posting them on my bedroom wall. These simple acts will remind me that I must go within myself for inspiration because that is where it resides. Silly me, I always forget this.

Evening:

Made it. This work-week is over. Thank goodness! I'm going to make breakfast for dinner. Don't want anything heavy. Watch some TV. This will be a productive and peaceful weekend. I claim it.

We're approaching Oakland City Station. 'Marvin Arrington' signs are everywhere. Huge signs that loom up over the street signs.

There's an adorable little guy sitting in his mom's lap directly behind the bus-driver. He reminds me of Ransom as a child, big almond shaped brown eyes. He's in a sky-blue snow-suit. Just adorable.

11/27/97
Journal Entry

I'm on Intake today but that's fine. Diet's coming along well, it's a lot of work. However, it's in keeping with my goal of saving by preparing and bringing my lunch. This takes time, next week I'm going to prepare stuff over the weekend to make it easier for the following week. Frankly, I'm enjoying what I'm eating and this is important to me. Certainly makes it easier to endure. I'm using honey in my coffee again, something I've been planning to get back into for quite some time.

It's thirty-eight degrees out this morning and it feel's fabulous! I'm dressed for it, two sweaters, my black and white pull-over and my old stand-by, a full-length, button down cardigan. This one I usually leave at work on the back of my chair for chilly days at the office. I also have on my bone-colored cape, the one my sister made for me years ago. She wouldn't believe that I still wear that thing, but it still looks good, it's in the way it hangs. The trick is to dress in layers in Atlanta, baby. It may be thirty degrees in the morning and rise to eighty-five by late afternoon. Seriously.

Lord, this bus moves so slow. So many stops to make. Not to mention the road construction around Honeysuckle Lane and Campbellton Road. And with all these clothes, I'm getting a little warm already. Speaking of which, I was slightly leery of leaving the house this morning right after jumping out of the shower, knowing my pores were still open. But I was running so late, didn't have a choice.

I've got to contact Ransom's attorney as he asked. Need to take another look at his letter first. The number and address is on there. Haven't sent him any money yet, either.

12/5/97
Journal Entry

My doggone tape recorder isn't working this morning. I'm out here on my way to the GAP training and this stupid tape recorder decides not to work. Of all the time for the batteries to die!

I'm thankful for this new day and with it a new spirit. I'll get the knowledge that's needed from this training session even without my tape-recorder, no need for anxiety.

Paul is going shopping this morning for food items, coffee and eggs, etc. We'll both go in the morning and do some real shopping at Kroger.

It's a glorious morning. Cool crisp air. Sun shining bright! Maybe I'll get to the Northwest office by 9:00 o'clock.

12/18/97
Journal Entry

Paul came in about 9:30 last night. He opened and closed the refrigerator a couple of times and then sat down at the dining-room table, making noises as if he didn't feel well. I'd been laying there clicking the remote back and forth from the Arts and Entertainment station to CNBC (for Heraldos' News show). I'd been dozing when he came in. Thank God he made it home safely. I said nothing to him, but got myself up and went upstairs to bed. Soon I heard pots and pans rattling, figured he was making himself hot dogs. Normally, I would have stayed alert to make sure he didn't leave the stove on or, worse, burn something when he comes in like this, but I went straight to sleep, exhausted.

My feet didn't hit the floor until after six this morning. A few stretches got me going. Made coffee and sat on the side of the bed for about fifteen minutes. Paul came up the stairs for a cigarette. As I stepped into the shower, I remembered that he had a VA appointment. When I finished showering and went down stairs, he was lying on the couch with his head covered with a throw.

"Are you going to the VA this morning? Don't you have an appointment?"

"I'm not going," he mumbled.

"That's just plain sorry," I snapped on my way back upstairs. Irritated and pressed for time, I said a few other choice things as well. Not long after, he entered the bathroom while I was doing my make-up, looking for a bar of soap. I gave him a bar and he headed to the downstairs bath.

"Are you going to VA then?" I yelled.

"Yeah, I'm going."

He wasn't quite ready when I left. I have to believe he's going, can't be sure. He went back upstairs after I came down. I prepared a salad to take for lunch with my left-over fried chicken.

This is Friday and I'm going to have a good day. Planning to shop for Christmas Dinner in the morning.

Later:

Went to Bankruptcy Court at 2:00 o'clock. Guess what? My attorney didn't show up! Seriously. He didn't show up! The judge shuffled some paper around, appeared to read a little here and there and finally said, between clenched teeth, "Have your attorney call me." I just can't believe it! I walked back to work and did a little, not much, I was too frustrated and just plain pissed off!

There's these teenagers on the train. Acting up and being rude as usual, using awful language. One is reading a letter aloud from some girl, just going on and on and bad-mouthing her.

We got an e-mail today regarding the Agency's Christmas Party. We're going to Pilgreen's Steakhouse in Jonesboro on Monday. The menu is T-bone steak or chicken and baked potatoes, etc. Supposedly, Pilgreen's is the best, hope so. I know I'll be doing the T-bone.

There's two young sisters across from me with two little girls with extension braids, extremely long and heavy-looking. These two women are talking loudly about courts and drugs and more drugs. The people in this city really try my nerves, both black and white. Right now I'm still seething thinking about that damn attorney not showing up! Didn't even have the decency to notify me!

I'm off for the weekend. I've got to get in touch with my joy, I know it's inside me somewhere!

We're creeping along on Campbellton Road, don't know why. Yes I do... it's Friday and the eagle flies. I can see folks darting between traffic to enter the liquor store across the street, and there's brothers gathered on the corner on the right dealing drugs right out in the open, taxi drivers stopping and starting, holding up traffic, competing for customers. Folks hustling and bustling shopping for Christmas at Campbellton Plaza, just living for the city, you know?

1/5/98
Journal Entry

Happy New Year! What a blessing to be here! It is warm and humid this morning. The weather-man said it was fifty-seven degrees earlier. Add the humidity factor and it feels like the high sixty's. I'm riding the # 83 with the wind blowing on the side of my face and I'm perspiring something crazy!

I can't discuss Christmas right now except to tell you that it was horrible! Paul went on a serious binge…his only excuse was that it was Christmas and he didn't feel like wallowing in his back pain which was more intense than usual and that the cocaine eases his pain considerably (he conveniently left out the part that the pain usually returns more intensely once he comes down). Me, I decided to hang out with my girl, Nita, and did some serious drinking.

Things took a change for the better on the last day of December when Paul's VA Disability claim was adjusted for increased compensation. Not 100% but considerably more than he's been getting. He's been fighting for this for many years so this news was huge. Both his Behavioral health Dr. and his Primary Care Dr. advised him that he would need to step up his attendance with NA meetings with VA as well as outside meetings, however. He's on cloud-nine right now. I'm glad for us both, financially. But… well, we'll see.

I'm on my way back to work after being off since Dec 24th. It doesn't seem as if I've been off that long. I'm glad to be going back. Strangely, I seem to handle more of my business when I'm working than when I have time off.

1/6/98
Journal Entry

I got a call late last night. Cindy's mother passed away yesterday. She hadn't been sick or anything until early yesterday, according to Cindy. Nita, Gail and I went over to the house. We stayed with her and her sister until 1:30 in the morning. My heart is with Cindy, she's so tender and giving. I didn't get to sleep until after 3:00 am. I'm tired. I will make the best of this day, however, and be thankful for each and every moment, life is so precarious, so unpredictable, you know?

I'm concerned about Ransom, my son. It appears as if he's still in the 'hole.' He wrote me last week with hopes of getting out in time for class on yesterday. He said he'd call over the weekend, but we haven't heard anything. I give it to the Lord, don't really know what in the world to do.

I got the East Point bus this morning. It's warm and muggy. Weatherman said it would be around 68 degrees. Can you believe it? With the humidity, it's quite warm.

There are some well-dressed women here on the train, looking uptight, as usual.

I've got to write Ransom. God bless that situation, please.

Later:

We went back over to Cindy's today for lunch. She's holding her own. She broke down once when someone called asking if her mom was feeling better, apparently not knowing that she'd died. Cindy hung up the phone quietly. Each of us hugged her as she began to cry. It's really hard, losing a loved one like that, especially your mother—so abrupt and unexpected! Needless to say, this has me thinking about my mom. I've got to get back up there to see her. I worry all the time that I can keep enough money put away to fly home at any given moment. Don't like to dwell on it but it's so important. The last time I spoke with her she sounded strong but confused. She gets Ransom and Keith mixed up. At other times she seems lucid.

Paula held the writers' group meeting at her place for the first time. She's converted half of her duplex into a little writer's colony of sorts. Her intention is for us to meet there on a regular basis. It's spacious and cozy, too. Great idea.

Hey, G, I know I spend lots of time complaining. I try to adjust to certain conditions and turn them around into something positive. That being said, not being a native of Atlanta, the oppressive heat, my personal problems and just surviving here is more than a passing notion! Often, in the past, it seemed as if everything was against us, Paul and me, I mean. But maybe we were against ourselves, going around in circles, never moving ahead. I'm ready to move forward now, G.

1/7/98
Journal Entry

G ood morning. Feeling good. Got a good nights' sleep last night. It's warm and humid this morning and the rain's still here. Love the rain. The humidity I'll just have to deal with.

Paul may get to the store this afternoon, depending on the rain.

I've got plenty of work to do this morning. Hope things go smoothly so that I can be prepared for tomorrow's interviews. Made a doctor's appointment yesterday.

Last night, I wrote a letter to Ransom's Warden. I'll re-write it today and mail it. I don't know if it will help or not, but it's worth a try.

Traffic is slow this morning due to the rain. People here don't drive well in the rain, very reckless!

They're still working on Campbellton Road. The orange and white cans and the orange cones and warning lights are still littered on the streets. There's no sign of any work crew. Even before the rain came, there hasn't been any workers out here for a while.

Man, I'm hungry this morning. But I need a good cup of coffee before I eat anything. That queasy feeling has crept back upon me. I am tired of feeling this way. Got to give up these cigarettes for good. I think they have plenty to do with it.

We're almost at Oakland City Station. If I can get on a schedule, I'd like to get out and catch the #82 East Point in the mornings and just get the 83 in the evenings. The East Point is much quicker getting to the station even though there's two additional stops on the train.

1/8/98
Journal Entry

I've got a full day ahead of me today. Scheduled appointments, letters to mail out. Monthly report still due. Oh, well, it's all in the game.

I was pleased to be able to fasten my navy slacks this morning. Usually, it's an effort and even after I've done so, they're so tight that I can't breathe. Obviously, these exercises are paying off. I'm going to begin doing them twice a day. Why not? To get where I want to be health-wise. I'm able to bite the bullet that way. Wish I could do the same with cigarettes. It's time to give them up and breathe healthily and deeply.

We've got another rainy day. I actually love the rain. There is something very peaceful in the sound of rain dropping on the roof tops. Looking out the window and watching everything washed clean. The trees, grass and plant-life being watered. It makes me feel very cared for. I always sleep well when it rains. It's somewhat different at the office, however. There, I look out my gigantic window and long to be home lounging in bed with a book or at least a good old movie. It's supposed to reach sixty-five degrees today. Feels that way already.

Angela Davis was on A&E last night. They were doing a segment about the FBI's most wanted list history. The first woman on that list was a woman from Honduros named Ruth Eisemann-Schier, who was charged with kid-napping for ransom. This was in 1968. A few years later, Angela Davis was placed on this list after she became involved with the Panthers and her body-guard killed someone. She was a bad sister. I will never forget her. She's still teaching in California. She's a Marxist, I believe. They don't make them as passionate and courageous as her anymore. Power to the People, my people!

1/12/98
Journal Entry

Well, Cindy buried her mother on Saturday. I found the funeral rather odd. Of course, it was the first funeral I've ever been to when the person is cremated. The service was held in the same building where the cremation was done. The casket was opened at the end of the service. Somehow it wasn't so sad, Mrs. Carlton actually looked quite good. Afterwards, we went back to the house with Cindy and her family and remained there for hours. Later, we went to Nita's for the little get-together that she'd planned. As it turned out, she didn't have the food prepared when we arrived and Joan and Gail teased and talked about her the entire night. I viewed this as just their way of lightening things up. But then we played Bid Whist and Joan began talking about me mercilessly. She really got on my nerves. I can't stand to lose. The only way to get her back was to kick her ass which I eventually did. She deserved it. She started in on Nita again and then Nita went into her bedroom and stayed forever while we played more cards and drank. Finally, when the game ended, I knocked on Nita's bedroom door to let her know we were leaving. She came out all apologetic and explained she'd been talking to, Chris, her man, but didn't elaborate. Once more, Gail commented on Nita's poor skills as a hostess and Nita actually laughed and we all relaxed and sat back down.

Nita's friend, Marian, is good people. Did I mention she was there? Well, anyway, she's from Milledgeville, Georgia, Nita's home town and they're old college buddies. She blended in, though I know she had to wonder about us, all the bitching and stuff. Anyway, at some point, she fired up a joint and I had a couple of hits. No one else did. Hope I don't have to hear about it again. Probably wasn't the wisest thing, I mean we're colleagues as well as friends but we don't usually get down like that. We all have our separate close friends that we hang out with, outside of the office and book club. I decided not to worry about it, and proceeded to enjoy myself. We drank plenty of cocktails, which is something we always do when we get together. As a result, I was tired as hell Sunday and stayed in bed until mid-afternoon.

I phoned Nita on Sunday after I couldn't reach Cindy. She was in bed and it was after five. She'd stayed up until 6 that morning after Chris came over.

We're approaching Garnett Station. Later.

Later:

Today wasn't so bad. Nita and I went to McDonald's for lunch and stopped and bought boot-leg Videos from a brother on the street. 'Amistad' and 'Jerry Springer Uncensored.'

Gail had 'The Jerry Springer Show' on her miniature TV when we got back to the office. We sat around and watched it for about 10 minutes. Just a bunch of nonsense, really.

This Bus Driver sits a long time at Oakland City Station. We're finally leaving---at 6:00 o'clock!

I know I need to get some rest tonight, but I do want to see these movies.

1/14/98
Journal Entry

I'm at East Point Station. Man, is this North-bound train taking forever or what? Just can't win as far as time is concerned. I left early this morning, expecting to get to work early or at least, on time.

WOW! I am really slipping! I forgot to enter anything about the Million Woman March experience! Why didn't you nudge me, G?! Oops, sorry, no disrespect intended. Not in your job description, too worldly, etc. Anyway, we went! Nita, Gail, Cindy, Joan and myself! A historical event! For those of you who live under a rock or just don't really give a damn, it was held in Philadelphia, Pa on Oct, 25 last year.

A local human rights advocate and Freedom fighter and owner of an African Crafts Shop, Phile Chionesu, put this thing together. It was all about family unity, black women in this country, sisterhood, hope, social change and economic change in the communities. In spite of the cold and rain, sisters came from across the country. They came in all manner of dress: jeans and T-shirts and hats, colorful African garb, all manner of hair-styles, mostly natural afros and braids and to keep it real, I must acknowledge that there were wig-wearing, extension-weave-wearing sisters as well. Hats, flags and conscious-raising T-shirts were everywhere! And the speakers! There was Attallah and Llyasah Shabazz, Malcolm X's daughters, Dr. Dorothy Height among other notable black women. Spiritually, mentally and physically, it was a blast, man! There were other heavy-hitter speakers too: Winnie Mandela, Congress woman, Maxine Waters, Sista Soldier and Jada Pinkett-Smith

(I personally found that amazing, had no idea Jada Pinkett was that socially conscious, even though I love her work). I remember Nita exclaiming ecstatically that she'd never seen so many black women coming together expressing themselves boldly and on common ground without an element of competition. She was in tears! We all were, tears of joy! Sisterhood for me wasn't unknown, after all, I came up in a household of females, worked in county government with sisters most of my adult life where we often came together and collectively wrote letters to our local representatives in support of increased wages and other local issues. Not only did we form an all-female Bowling league for our County, but we founded an all-female Pool players (billiard players) league, which was great fun because we were welcomed in pool-halls around the city (to play for free) because we weren't taken seriously until we demonstrated that we were kick-ass players! But these experiences are greatly diminished by the 'Million Woman March!' We left that experience 'fired up' and ready to take on life with an exuberance and vitality that neither of us had experienced before. Each of us vowed to have more empathy for our clients, volunteer more, choose more meaningful books for the book club and be more supportive of family and each other as a sisterhood.

I'm at East Point Station. Man, is this North-bound train taking forever or what?

Yesterday was interesting. After Paul and I had a disagreement on the phone (about money, of course), he had a change of mind and didn't press the issue. He even stayed home. This morning, he said he had a crisis yesterday. Said he would have been pissed off if he'd gone to VA tomorrow and been tested for drugs and came up dirty. I know that's true. I brought it up yesterday, too. But normally he doesn't listen to me. Guess he didn't give in to that monkey on his back. That he's putting forth an effort to stay clean is what's important, regardless of the motivator. Anyway, that's what I tell myself. I realize that I'm an enabler because sometimes I empathize with him, knowing that the cocaine eases his chronic pain. When he goes on a binge, he has no pain for days after.

Today went well overall. I had seven Intake cases, but only two of them were TANF's. I finished the last one at 2:11 pm. Then, I rushed to the meeting in Room 219 on DOL bullshit. A lot of noise about communicating with each other about the clients. She even had the audacity to suggest that we complete the DOL applications for the client! At that point I couldn't sit still. I mean that's probably the only form that the client has to complete. Just no way, man! Anyway, I did my best to be diplomatic by not speaking on all the things we have to do. I'm sure most of my colleagues appreciated what I said. The meeting went on until almost 4:00 o'clock. Thank goodness, I don't have any appointments tomorrow. Should be able to catch up on some of those cases I've been holding and haven't had time to complete. First I'll complete those three or four TANF cases that I interviewed on the 5th or whatever day it was.

1/15/98
Journal Entry

G ood morning, G. Thanks for remaining at my side, I can feel you. Thanks to the Creator for another day in this wonderful/crazy life! I got up early and got a head-start on the day. Did some sit-ups and stretching for thirty minutes, felt good. It's payday. Paul has an appointment at VA this morning. He's doing better... he feels that he is. I know that he is but I'm not so sure about myself. (G, please help me with this fear and dread that I feel). I'm hoping I have enough to do the things that I want to do this pay. My bank account only had $651.00 this morning. I withdrew $200.00. That can't be right, is it? So what I'm hoping is that Winn Dixie's check has been paid. Praise God. Enough of the self-pity already.

On the light side, this is my last day of the week. I'm off tomorrow and Monday. Also, I'll get to work early this morning. This damn train is packed to the max. Unbelievable, this time of the morning! People standing all in the isle, hovering over each other. Never seen it like this, early in the morning. I hear a brother behind me complaining. He had the same idea, get to work early, get an early start.

I certainly need a second cup of coffee this morning.

1/18/98
Journal Entry

Thank you, Most Magnificent Creator, for the formation of all things great and small! Morning G! Thanks for your presence. I have all that I need. If only I could keep this front and center in my head, regardless of how things appear.

Well, work has truly been trying in the past few weeks. Constant interviews, both Intake and Ongoing as well as Walk-ins. Computer issues, stress and confusion among colleagues. You name it, it has really been something! Yet even as I speak about these things, I understand that I am fortunate to have a job. There are many who don't and our current administrators seem hell-bent on keeping us aware of this and dammit, I resent it. The mind games. Yet... it is true. There are those who would feel fortunate to have a decent gig/career and who would gladly look over these issues. I know I need to keep things in perspective.

We're at East Point Station.

Keith called last night. He says Patrice is pregnant. Just wonderful! They are truly being blessed. He also scolded me for not calling him to say happy birthday. Now that was really an over-sight. One that has never happened before! Can't begin to convey how I felt. Father, please help me to stay in the present, that I may not be so overwhelmed with job responsibilities and personal issues that I fail to remember things like this. I love my kids too much for that.

2/10/98
Journal Entry

I've been wearing this 'Patch' to quit smoking since yesterday. Don't think I can do it, however. I don't like the way the nicotine feels as if it's cursing through my veins! Seriously! And I'm having problems sleeping at night. I should say, this is aggravating the problem I already have getting to sleep. Geesh!!

Clayton died the end of last month. God, I hate using that word! It's so unreal. There is no way that he is gone! It hurt so much to think about it. Everything's been sort of foggy since we found out. He was not only Pauls' best friend, but he was the brother I never had. Man, it would have been great for him to see Paul doing better! I can't forget how he told me to 'save myself' because he felt that Paul was bringing me down. Believe me, it moved me when he first said that to me. Because I know that even though he loved me, Paul was like his brother, and he was every bit as devastated as I was with Pauls' situation. He had distanced himself considerably from us, not coming around on weekends like he used to. Oh, man, my heart is broken. I haven't even called Pat yet, her and Green moved out to Arizona, so she doesn't know. I really can't even write about this right now. Maybe later.

Anyway, this smoking thing is a trip. Right now, I'm conflicted. I know I really want to quit. I really need help with this. If only my sinus's would clear up or something. God, I'm tired. And why do I only have $45.00 in my checking account. What's up with that?

2/11/98
Journal Entry

Headed to Five Points Station. We've got P-Jam Training at the Northwest Office this morning. Gail, Linda and I, that is. Mandy is supposed to be there also. Guess we're the bad girls since we haven't been P-Jamming hardly since the program was implemented.

I'm still not smoking. Had one cigarette this morning. The effort feels good, believe me, I really do want to be smoke-free. But as far as 'the Patch' is concerned, I simply can't handle it, how it makes me feel, can't deal with it!

I hope to do more work on my poems before our Writers' Group convenes this Saturday. It would be nice to read them aloud to the group.

2/18/98
Journal Entry

I've been working really well this week, trying to catch up. Scheduled my appointments for Monday and Tuesday of next week, which is cutting it close, but what're you going to do? I was off an entire week, the first week of this month. Filing, Transfer cases, Specials, everything has piled up! But Mandy's off the rest of the week. That helps. Won't have to be giving her constant updates or worry about being pulled to do other stuff, so I can buckle down. I'm on Intake on Friday, however. Geez!

2/19/98
Journal Entry

Feeling good this morning. Second day on 'the Patch.' Remember, I got off of it last week after the third day. It doesn't feel as strange as it did last week. Maybe able to do it. My nasal passages feel clearer. Also, I'm pleased with myself for sticking with my exercises. Also, I dance along with the work-out to music every morning (I've got some awesome music, baby! Treasure my R&B and Jazz collection, it speaks to who I am, defines me). It's exhilarating. Then I shower and prepare for work. It's beginning to show. My waist and stomach is noticeably tighter. And... I've lost a few pounds and my legs are stronger. Oh, and I walk as much as possible. Linda and I've started walking in the afternoon, again. She's very motivating, doesn't have an ounce of fat anywhere on her body, but she's very health-conscious. I need that.

We're leaving East Point Station. This is much better than Oakland City. The wait isn't as long and it's not nearly as crowded. It's Thursday, only one more day, thank God.

Weather is gorgeous, not cold at all. We're supposed to get rain tonight, though, according to the morning weather-woman.

I've simply got to write Pat, or call her and let her know about Clayton's death. I keep putting it off, can't bring myself to talk about it. I feel some kind of way, knowing she would have contacted me right away if things were the other way around, I'm sure. I'm trifling like that, I don't know.

I'm late and on Intake this morning. I did call in. A client is waiting on me this very moment. I give this day to my Higher Self. Thanks for all of our blessings, Father. Thanks for keeping Paul safe from harm and sending him home today in good physical and emotional health. Thanks for continually blessing my children and their families and extended family members as well. Thanks for my smoke-free status and physical fitness. All blessings, indeed. Help us to persevere. You're the Keeper of all Joy and all Good. Thank You for sharing these gifts with us. Amen.

4/2/98
Journal Entry

Morning, G.

I'm an emotional wreck this morning. Fear and dread is over-taking me. Physically, I'm alternating between too much food, caffeine and cigarettes. Just awful! Combine that with my procrastination with my writing assignment.

Paul left the house yesterday morning and hasn't returned. Yes, he called yesterday evening. The conversation was strange, nothing much was said. I asked him where he was but I don't recall his response. At the time my mind was racing, over-come with anger. There were voices in the background. I assume he was in the usual location. He was mostly silent, just holding the phone. He kept saying 'I'll call you later' in a subdued tone. Most likely, he was paranoid. He gets that way when he's out there in those streets binging, but I wasn't thinking about this when he called. "Are you coming in or are you going to stay out there? I've had it with this, Paul. Either come in or stay out there!" (I'm beginning to sound like a broken record even to myself).

'I'll call you." And of course he didn't. So here we are again; me hoping and praying that he's okay and on the other hand trying to convince myself that I no longer care. God, help us please!

I'm out here on the #83, trying to make it to work. It'll be after nine by the time I get there. Praying for miracles. Feeling very weary.

Well, I've gotten it all out. Now I can go positive. I've trained my mind to do that. Switch channels. Next. I bless this day with all of my goodness, with full knowledge that things will work out, not only in personal matters but my work… the tremendous volume of stuff I've got to get done in the next three days, as well as my health. I place all negative thoughts surrounding these issues in the hands of the Holy Spirit. Amen.

4/15/98
Journal Entry

We're supposed to do the radio show this Friday, providing the Freak-nickers don't shut everything down with all that traffic. Also, the coffee house where our group has been meeting has agreed to provide us with a larger room. Isn't that great, G?! I haven't been participating as much as I'd like, but hopefully that's going to change.

We're approaching Garnett Station in a minute. Be talkin.' It's time to get myself back on track now.

4/22/98
Journal Entry

I t's Wednesday. Out here rolling on the #83. They've got Barge Road over there by Sun Trust Bank all torn up. Men at work. Guess they're widening that road also. Whatever they're doing, I promise you it's going to take forever.

Paul says he passed out this morning. I heard a loud noise as if something had fallen as I was getting dressed. I called out to him. "Paul, are you all right?"

"Yeah, I'm okay," he answered. I barely heard him, the radio was playing and I was preoccupied, getting myself together. When I came downstairs a few minutes later, he asked me why I'd asked if he was alright.

"I heard something falling or something." I said.

"I was standing at the sink, getting ready to get some coffee, thinking how tired I felt and I began to feel dizzy. The next thing I knew, you were calling me asking if I was alright and I was on the floor, all dizzy and shit!" That upset me, big-time.

"That's it, you're going to the VA and get checked out," I said.

"Naw, I'm alright. Last night was the first night I started back on my sleeping pills. That's all." He sounded pretty certain. We finally agreed that he would cancel the dental appointment he already had with the dental hygienist at VA. It was raining and threatening a storm, anyway. Fix it, Jesus!

Hope I can accomplish something this morning. I really need to work straight through all day, but we've got Staff Appreciation scheduled for this afternoon. I know the idea is for us to appreciate the break and try to enjoy it. But when you're over-whelmed with pending work and the end of the month is approaching, not to mention the Window Period, it doesn't help much! Oh well, such is life.

Father, bless this day and all that it contains. I'm still expecting that miracle. Good health. Financial freedom.

Joan Johnson gave me some Zantac today. My stomach was hurting just that bad. I've got a prescription for Tagamet, maybe I'll pick it up Thursday at Eckert's in East Point.

Man did I get lucky a minute ago! I got off of the East Point train, ran up the stairs just in time to catch the #82. We're rolling now. It's all good. Sure hope my income taxes came. I've got a lot to try and handle.

4/29/98
Journal Entry

I'm out here rolling on the #83 to Oakland City. Left the house at 7:15. God is good. Been saying my prayers morning and night in the last few days.

Paul came in this morning around 6:00 o'clock. He didn't appear all bent out of shape as expected. It took everything in me not to say anything to him, everything's already been said. It's a season of doing now. Lord…please give us the victory.

I'm pleased to get to work a little early even though I didn't leave the office until seven yesterday. This is the end of the month and there's still plenty to do. We've got a conference this afternoon at the Northwest office at 2:00 o'clock. I'll have to get out of the office at one at the latest.

G, you must have put in a good word for me, I feel good this morning. My anxiety has abated somewhat. This evening, my goal is to work on my writing assignment as well as Ransom's letter. It really is amazing that I haven't been able to concentrate on either for the past two weeks.

I cut my braids Monday. They look quite together now. They were just too long, hanging in my face and all, was irritating.

I've been taking vitamins (stress tabs) for a couple of days, my system is beginning to feel better. Also, I'm taking calcium regularly. My health is very important to me at this time. I continue to exercise regularly, not every morning, but rarely less than four days a week. My smoking is the only thing that I'm not in control of at this point. But with the Creator's help, I'll overcome soon. I try not to beat up on myself. I really want to get into Yoga this summer.

There can't be enough said about the power that comes from keeping a journal. It's a spiritual thing for me.

Later:

Got plenty done this morning. Before I knew it, it was time to leave for the EBT conference. It was okay. It only went from 2:00 until a little after 3:00 pm. Staff began leaving after the first demonstration on the system. I didn't hesitate to leave either, one can only take so much. The good thing about the Northwest Office is its' location. It sits right next to the Bankhead Train station, actually, this location is named 'the Bankhead office. Anyway, I just walked out and got on the train. Sweet. Much of the staff that works at this office drive their cars to the nearest train station and take the train to the office, saving much wear on their cars, not to mention gas money.

It's getting crowded on this bus and we seem to be sitting longer than usual. Oh, kids are getting out of school. Thank goodness it's not hot yet, I'm not looking forward to commuting in the heat.

Wow, we were just directed to jump off of the #82 as another one screeched around the corner! Apparently, there was a problem with the other one. No one will tell you anything. You would think the driver would make an announcement or something. That's too much like right, I guess. Just let you sit there wondering what the hell is going on! Whatever. Now, this one is flying out of the station like he stole something!

It's been quite cloudy all day, we may get rain before the day ends. That will be fine with me, especially at bedtime.

4/30/98
Journal Entry

There. Made the last day of the month. Didn't do bad either. Got most of my work done. Only left six FS Certifications. I registered those for after the 15th of the month. Cleaned up pretty good. I'm glad this month's over. Next month I hope to get my office better organized so that I can deal with whatever is coming up. We've got changes galore still going on and more conferences, meetings and training sessions still to be scheduled. So I've got to prepare as best I can.

I've got to write my son, Ransom and Rosie as well. She's been on my mind since yesterday. I just feel like saying something more to her about Clayton's death. She's his sister. We spoke briefly at his funeral but haven't connected since. I really like her, she has the same kind and compassionate nature as Clayton.

Man, these stations pop up quickly when I'm writing. I know it doesn't take long, but really, when you're preoccupied, the time really flies.

Looks like it's going to rain again this evening. No surprise. The weatherwoman has predicted rain for most of the week.

Hope I can get to work early again and complete my Monthly Report on time.

Looks like a storm is brewing out there.

A woman just got into a Marta Police car. She got in the front seat and the officer sped away. Couldn't tell if there was trouble or not. Another officer stood aside near his vehicle watching them. He remained there a while and then walked into the station.

I ate too much today. For breakfast I finished off my hot wings. At lunch I had three slices of pizza. This was all left over from yesterday's dinner from Pizza Hut. My stomach still doesn't feel as bad as it has, though. But I think I need to cut back. All of the exercises I'm doing is good but my appetite is really out there!

We're on the #82 and just about to reach my destination... home.

5/1/98
Journal Entry

TGIF, as they say. It's been a grueling week, but I got through it. I'm out here rolling on the #83 on my way to the office. I finally finished the letter to the Judge on Ransom's behalf and got it out. Also, did most of my writing assignment. My goal for the weekend is to clean the apartment, put my important papers and poems in order and finish my writing. I will begin with the writing. I'm always putting it last and often don't get around to it.

Paul promised that he'd call me this morning to meet me and give me some money. He didn't call. I'll make it. I'm not going to trip. I give it to the Most-High, right, G? Right now, I am free from despair and want to remain so. I don't know when I will see him or if he's alright. But he'll survive, always does. God got him. Right now, I'm trying to stay in the present.

I'm getting better with this timeliness thing. For some time now, I've left home at a more reasonable time. I'm up early again, exercising, praying/meditating and all that good stuff. Feels good.

I'm expecting nothing but miracles. I understand that I must be miracle-minded in order to see them.

5/3/98
Journal Entry

I didn't sleep at all last night. As a result I read most of 'The Millionaire Next Door.' I can see why it made the best-seller list. There's some great information in there in spite of all of the graphs and statistic. Anyway, I came away with the conclusion that I needed to 'downsize' as the suits say. Based on our income, we should be living in a cheaper place, no getting around it. Especially because it is rent and we get no return. Later, Gator.

5/5/98

G ot out just in time to get the #82 this morning. I lay in bed until after 6. G, my heart is truly heavy this morning. Do you hear me, G? Please help me. My eyes are blood red from crying. Got my shades on, G. 'Lil' Clayton is dead. We're still missing his dad something awful, and now he's gone. It's crazy, G. I got a call from Fulton County's Coroner's office...the Coroner's office at work the day before yesterday! I panicked the minute the female identified herself, she had to repeat herself several times. Finally, I made myself listen as she explained that my address was listed as his last known address or whatever. That call is still not quite clear, but, bottom line they wanted me to come down and identify the body! That really messed me up. She wouldn't give me any details. She wanted to know if I was related and or knew of his nearest relative. I fumbled for my phone book and finally gave her Clayton's mom's address in upstate New York. She hung up abruptly after getting that information. I sat there stunned, unable to move or gather myself, barely able to breathe. We couldn't get any more information until yesterday. Marsha, his mom, called yesterday after she flew in and identified him. She was told that he was in an accident on I-85. They said the accident wasn't that serious, but he must have panicked because he jumped from his SUV and commenced to run through traffic screaming and yelling like a madman...that's what they said. Said once the officers subdued him and confiscated his vehicle, drugs were found and he resisted arrest. Claims he wrestled with one of the officers, attempting to get his gun, said they had to shoot him. They shot him five times. Killed him. Claim it was self-defense and they are deeply sorry. Marsha is inconsolable. We are crushed. How could this happen? How?

Marsha sent 'Lil' Clayton here to his father, Clayton Sr., a few years ago to get him off the streets of New York. She could no longer handle him. Said he was hanging out with gangs, getting into trouble and disrespecting her. She also found a gun in his bedroom and when she confronted him, he went off on her. She said he's been angry since she and his father divorced years ago. He blamed her for it all and said he'd rather be with his father. She gave in and sent him here as soon as he graduated high school. Clayton Sr. was glad to have him with him and for a while things were good. Tension soon developed between them, however. 'Lil' Clayton didn't like the idea that his dad was working in a factory here in Atlanta. After all, in New York, Clayton had worked in banking, had done well financially. This is where he and Paul met many years ago. Clayton explained to his son that it was difficult getting back in that groove in Atlanta and that after having a heart attack he didn't really want to even if he was able. He told him he enjoyed working in production at Atlanta Journal & Constitution. It was good for him physically and much less stressful. 'Lil' Clayton didn't understand this. Soon he began disrespecting Clayton and telling him he wasn't shit. It got ugly and the handwriting was on the wall. After a year or so, Clayton threw him out. He told us he really didn't want to but he couldn't stand the way 'Lil' Clayton looked at him. He could see the distain and disrespect in his son's eyes and it hurt. Paul tried talking to 'Lil' Clayton one day about the way he was disrespecting his dad. 'Lil Clayton told him that he had more respect for him (Paul) even though he was an addict, than he did his father. Said at least he wasn't a sell-out. He wouldn't take some menial job and shit. Paul didn't like that. There was no way he could share this conversation with Clayton, so he left it alone and when Clayton questioned him how things had gone when he spoke with 'Lil' Clayton he simply told him "I couldn't reach him man, let him go, turn him over to God. He's a grown man." Soon we learned that 'Lil' Clayton was dealing drugs…quite successfully. After learning this Clayton cut him off completely until 'Lil' Clayton caught a case for shooting someone. This young brother stole drugs and money from him, so he found him on the street and shot him, didn't kill him, but 'Lil' Clayton went to prison. Clayton shelled out a lot of money for a lawyer to take his case. He just gave away thousands of dollars for nothing. 'Lil' Clayton did ten years. Clayton died before 'Lil' Clayton got his freedom. He had continued heart issues since having his heart attack, but I believe something in him broke when he couldn't help his son. They wouldn't even allow 'Lil' Clayton a release to go to his dad's funeral. Marsha tried to arrange it, but things fell through.

5/6/98
Journal Entry

Morning, G

Spoke with Keith last night. I'm going down to Huntsville and spend Mother's Day weekend with them. I'll take a vacation day on Monday. To hell with worrying about all the work to be done. It's not going anywhere. I need a break. And Paul will be alright. It will be so good to see them.

I couldn't go on about 'Lil' Clayton yesterday, my heart was too heavy. Marsha came over late last night, she needed to talk. She talked and we cried and she talked some more. Lord, we've got to plan and get through this funeral, G.

Evening:

Made it through another day. I traded intake days with Robert Davis yesterday. I took his turn today and he's taking mine tomorrow. Wasn't too bad. I had all Food Stamp Certifications, no TANF's or Medicaid. But at one point, Nita had all Combo's. Three in a row. She asked me to take one and I refused. She was upset. She confronted me later this afternoon. After she ran it down, I realized one of the Combo's should have been mine. But at the time she asked me to take one, I thought they were rightfully hers. Whatever, I was wrong so I'm glad we cleared the air. It's interesting that she mentioned more than once that she thought we were 'tight' like that! Which leaves me to believe that she doubts my sincerity or my friendship or something. As though

I'd really let her down. Am I that hard to read? Or, am I so wishy-washy that I can't make myself clear? What? No one else sees me that way… that I know of. I didn't mean to make her feel bad. The thing is, I was caught up into what I had to do and 'Lil' Clayton kept flashing in my mind and also she was so abrupt in the first place (she's always that way). I told her that it wasn't personal, that I hate Intake and that my first inclination was to say 'no.'

I just saw a house up here on Headland Dr. with a 'For Sale sign from Century 21. If you're going toward the train station, the house is a little after you pass that elementary school. It's a brick house, not real big. Didn't see much, but I'd like to.

5/7/98
Journal Entry

Morning, G

Well, it's Thursday, my last working day for the week. Thank God for small things. I tried not to get emotional this morning as Paul began talking about 'L

il' Clayton's up-coming funeral and how we needed to be strong for Marsha. He was preparing to go to VA to pick up some important papers and I knew it would be the most natural thing in his world to make a detour and disappear for a few days and medicate to avoid showing up for his best friend's son burial. This thought unnerved me for a moment but then I decided I had no control over this, whatever happens, happens. I know I will be there. The Creator is still in control. I'm going to make the most of this day, G.

There are some wonderful faces on this train. I've got to begin looking closely at things again. Noticing detail. Describing it. Isn't that what reality is about anyway? So it must be that a writer comes to appreciate life through her ability to examine and interpret things in an interesting and expressive manner to get her audience's attention. So I not only look at scenery as I ride the train, but I observe expressions, a flash of color, a twinkle in an eye, the rust on the side of the train, you know, G? The darting eyes of the odd-looking character near the back…what's on his mind? Is he up to something?

We're rolling on the southbound train to East Point station. From here I can see the #82 is already there, ready to roll. Later.

5/12/98

Well, G, somehow we got through the funeral yesterday. A sad affair. A mother burying her only child.

Marsha appeared calm but I know she was completely exhausted both emotionally and mentally. Paul and I sat side by side (yes he made it) crying. Him for the loss of his dear friends' child, me for the loss of a young man who had become like another son to me. I sat there remembering how he'd come and sit down at my feet in the living room after Paul fell asleep and say, "Talk to me auntie." He and I both loved smooth jazz so we would get that going, and I would let him talk. He always talked about growing up in New York, how he dreamed of being a rapper. He even shared some of his lyrics with me and I thought they were good. It was positive stuff, the kind they don't often play on the radio stations, but never-the-less has a following. Told me how he missed his dad during those days. Sometimes he would bring Brandy or Rum and we'd sip while I made his favorite hot wings and salad with Ranch dressing, which we both liked. His favorite saying was, "Why don't you just keep it real, auntie, forget the salad and just dip the wing down in the dressing!" And so I did, and it was good. When he got his dad's life insurance, which turned out to be a huge sum, (he also received his father's inheritance from property that their family owned in Aruba) he brought me his bank books to hold on to while he sorted out what he was going to do. I held on to them tightly, Paul never knew, I didn't tell him until after 'Lil' Clayton purchased a home in College Park and collected them from me. He paid hard cold cash for the house. It broke my heart that he never got to spend one night in that house. 'Lil' Clayton was tough as they come and keenly intelligent on so many levels and he was also loving and lovable if you got to know him. Yes,

I did love him and so did Paul. He spent one Christmas weekend in jail to keep Clayton from getting arrested again while he was still on probation… that's a whole other story. God, I will never forget him. Seems like yesterday that Paul had written Ransom a letter asking him to write Clayton Jr. "I feel like he can impart some knowledge of what he's gone through, how he's gotten to this point with the system," he'd said. "It could be helpful to both of them to communicate with each other, their situations are just about the same, you know, even though Ransom didn't hurt anyone," he'd said.

5/14/98
Journal Entry

Morning, G
All praises to the Most High
It's going to be a nice day today
On the Train. There's a brother rapping about life:

They don't care anything about nothin' but money. Don't care nothin' bout no God or nothing.' And looka here, look at this obituary here. They leavin here, I'm tellin' you, look at this; 28 years old, 22 years old. They leavin here. And them Undertakers, oh yeah. They makin the money, okay. They makin the money. Them old preachers, boy, when folks die they get all that money, too. They attend those funerals, too. Preach, preach like a Mo Fo. Those undertakers… they fix those faces up. I'm talkin old men, young women, you name it. Them undertakers makin Money!"

Such is life riding Marta. I'm staring at the sign at the front of the train; 'Ride Marta, It's Smarta!' I'm shaking my head.

Later:

Out here rolling on the southbound to East Point Station. Just left work and it's going on 8:00 pm! Got the bright idea around 5:30 to re-arrange my office. Actually, I enjoyed it. Worked up a little sweat, got it looking a little neater. Anyway, I did get a Food Stamp case completed.

The #82 just pulled up at 7:45. The driver told a female passenger that he will be here until 8:10. Typical. So what are you going to do?

It's hot as hell sitting here! I've got to relax to get the perspiration under control. Sometimes, I think I'm actually hyper-ventilating… it's like a mind-over-matter thing, breathe-relax, breathe-relax, you know, just to calm down!

Seinfeld's last show is on tonight. Should be fun, going to be an hour long, I think. Hope I can get home in time to watch it. Going to try and get some rest tonight. I'm always over-extending myself one way or the other. If I'm not convincing myself that I can solve someone else's problems, I'm over-doing it at the office. I should be writing poems and creating magic and beauty, right, G? I've got to do better. I give thanks for this day, though.

5/15/98
Journal Entry

I've been praying. Read part of Genesis last night. First time I've read the bible in quite some time, G. I read the entire thing many years ago. I skipped over some of the 'begets'...who begat who, you know, which is pretty important, but I found it so tedious! I'm continually in prayer for Paul and to see this cycle of addiction broken, however.

5/28/98
Journal Entry

Trip to Huntsville was nice. Keith and his wife, Carol fill me with pride. They're both extremely industrious. I think reality has finally set in, though. He's begun talking about money and how they've over-consumed. He says they can't make any new purchases for the next couple of years. Learning and growing, it seems.

Yesterday went well. Accomplished quite a bit at the office, then at home, began my writing assignment which I expect to finish this evening.

6/8/98
Journal Entry

Out hear rolling on my way to the writer's group, Urban Colony Writer's, we call ourselves. Missed the #83 to get there on time, which means I missed Morris and Betty at Oakland City Station. I had the forethought to call the Coffee House. Mona was just getting there so I told her to ask Morris if he'd pick me up at Eastlake Station. Now that I think of it, I may be able to walk from there. Geez!

An interesting thing happened after I missed the bus. A low-to-the ground sister dressed in red pants and top came out of Sun Trust Bank, struggling with a walking-cane, and asked me about bus #83. We struck up a conversation. Immediately, she began telling me her troubles. I gave her my attention because she seemed pleasant enough. Her live-in partner took money from her checking account last week. Three hundred and ten dollars to be exact. As a result, she's been trying to come up with enough money to pay her rent. Yesterday, she was told by management at her complex that her rent would not be accepted. She was devastated, of course. Making matters worse, she's just had hip-surgery a couple of weeks ago. She said she put him out yesterday and that she'd just signed an affidavit stating she didn't write the check. She was telling my story! Killing me softly with it!

6/9/98
Journal Entry

O ut here rolling on the south-bound train to East Point, headed home. Accomplished a lot today. Worked on Specials most of the day. Got more, but the bulk of them are done. I'll finish them tomorrow, complete over-payments, transfer new cases and then start completing reviews.

I have no money to speak of, but the rent is paid. This is tiresome and boring and fills me with anger. I really try and I pray, too. I'm trusting in the Creator to work it out because I believe in prayer. But sometimes it seems as if the world is wrong-side out. The whole thing.

This train is extremely loud, don't know why everybody appears all fired up. Two young men up front, hand-slapping and high-fiving everything each says. Other young brothers in the back going on and on non-stop. And the motor is super-loud, probably a really old one which needs servicing! This elderly woman next to me is quiet and looks tranquil and calm. I'm always quiet. Try to keep my distance commuting out here, you never know who's who. People can be rather crazy, you know. But I do try to be pleasant enough to acknowledge folk when they speak to me. Some you regret speaking to, while others whom you imagine you'd love to talk to avoid you. There aren't many of these, however.

6/12/98
Journal Entry

Made this day, thanks to the Most High. We had a county-wide meeting this afternoon.

It held my interest. Ronald Stevens spoke about how the error rate has declined in Eligibility. He heaped praises on us and on his favorite people in Child Protective Services. I love Ronald Stevens because he first loved us. He's a good man.

6/15/98
Journal Entry

Do you ever stop to think about the Magnificence of the Creator, G? The Author of all things? The Artist of the Sun, the Moon and the Stars! Oops, I guess you do, no disrespect, G. Anyway, I'm feeling gratitude today, G. All praises to the Most High. Please help me that I may know my worth. Thank You and Amen.

Paul came home late Saturday night. I was feeling hopeless but determined. I'd decided that he absolutely had to go. There's been so much negativity going on. But get this, he came in with a resolution:

"I'm through with the stuff," he said. "I'm through. I was shown something yesterday." He went on to explain that he'd gone off on the young dope boys.

"What do you mean, you went off on them?"

"I mean, I lost it. I told them how they ain't shit. How they treat junkies like they ain't shit! How they don't know how to manage their money. How they exploit and use their own people, how they don't care about their own neighborhood. They ain't shit!"

I could only stare at him. The incongruity of it all.

"This brother took me to Morrow, Ga and showed me something. This brother got a crib like you wouldn't believe, man! Wall-to-wall TV, everything you could want in a house. Brother got four kids and a wife. Kids all manageable and respectable. He's dealing from a little shack off of 285. Nothing but white boys jumping off the interstate. Buying that shit like it's gold! Twenty-four-seven! Know what I'm sayin? Every five minutes, white boys pulling up in the drive. They don't even have to get out of their cars. They pull up, throw up their fingers, man. Dope boy runs to the car, they exchange hands. White boy is out of there. Cops ride through, periodically. Nobody gets arrested, nobody goes to jail! As long as they keep it quiet. As long as there's no carnival atmosphere and shit, you know? Noise and brothers up and down the street fighting over who's next in line to make a sale and shit. It ain't like that. See, the white boys, they're gonna get what they want. You understand what I'm sayin? Cops ain't gonna take them to jail. They gonna let them get what they want! You don't believe that, do you?

It's true, man! And that's the way to go, sell it to them. Stop devastating our neighborhoods. Stop selling it to our people. Sell it to them motha fuckus!"

"How could you say that, though, Paul?" I was actually trembling with anger. "How could you even consider that? Look what it's done to you? How could you wish that on anyone, black, white or brown?" I didn't even bother to speak on the fact that he would have to get clean first! He sounded like a special kind of fool!

"Look what they've done to us. Look at slavery. Look how things are now. Look how they put the shit in our neighborhoods, man!" He gestured with his hands. "This ain't no joke. This ain't no movie, man. This is real life. Why shouldn't we sell it to them, twenty-four-seven? Look what they've done to us, man!"

I could see where he was coming from, but my knee-jerk rational response was, well, two wrongs don't make a right. What I said was this; "You can't change the past, you've got to deal with the present, current situation. And if you're going to stop using, you've got to remove yourself from that environment all together. You're delusional, Paul!"

6/29/98
Journal Entry

Been awhile, hasn't it, G? A lots been happening. Ransom got what sounds like some positive feed-back from the judge. Right now, we're just waiting. I asked Paul to call Ransom's attorney this morning. Who knows whether he'll reach anyone. Speaking of Paul, I didn't put him out. We've been doing a lot of talking and he's managed to stay clean the last couple of weeks. We've been concentrating on the finances, trying to stay above water. I agreed to let him stay for now. Go figure!

I'm going to be late this morning, but as long as I get there before the staff meeting. I certainly hope our little baby-girl from CPS is okay. On Friday, a mother of one of our CPS children attempted to kill her child. Right up the street from the office. Somehow, she managed to sneak the child out of the office (don't ask me how she did it, they keep it pretty secure in that dept.) after getting angry when she learned that the child was not going to be released into her custody. Me, Nita and a CPS Supervisor caught up with her on the little bridge up the street and attempted to take the child. At that point, the mother began twisting the baby's head around while holding her out over the bridge threatening to drop her! "Back off, bitches, back off!" She snarled like an animal. I'm choking up just thinking about it. Long story short, Nita gently talked her into placing the child in her arms just as Atlanta's Finest arrived on the scene. I could hardly breathe. The tension was horrific! Man!

7/7/98
Journal Entry

It has been a very long weekend. For one thing, Paul went out... took one of the TV's with him. When he called in the wee hours, I told him not to come back. Period. Saturday, I went to church with Malcolm and his wife. It was interesting to say the least. The sermon was centered around a young girl who had been missing. When I got home from church, Paul had kicked the door in and was fast asleep in bed. I called the police. They made him leave but not before they lectured me on Georgia law. The long and short of it is they can't force him out since he's a resident in the home and receives his mail there. I will have to have him evicted in order to remove him. So much for protection under the law. What if he were violent, for heaven's sake! I can only thank God he hasn't been. But isn't kicking a door in an act of violence? (He's going to fix that damn door, too!). Saturday night, I went to Cindy's cook-out, it was a blast, a real stress-buster. Something I needed. I didn't get home until after 5:00 am Sunday morning. By 6:00 am, Paul started calling me. At first I ignored him, but he kept calling. Finally, I relented, knowing he had no place to go and wasn't going to let up and also because I was totally exhausted, I let him come over. He promptly fell asleep on the chair and I went back to bed. Later in the afternoon we had a long talk. It was difficult. I tried to tell him how tired I am and that I can't carry him any longer. Then he said, "I need a friend." This was new. I felt it. He reminded me of the times back in the day when I was having problems and drinking excessively and how he was always there for me. I reminded him that I didn't exactly descend into alcoholism even though I was an emotional mess.

"That's irrelevant," he said. "You were drinking like one. Do you know how much I hate drunkenness? It makes me sick to my stomach (his mother was an alcoholic, G). But even when you were pissy-drunk, crying and calling on me, I was there. I was always there." What he said was true. However, there is a tremendous difference in the time frame for the period he's speaking of and the time period I've been going through this addiction with him. It's been years. I pointed this out to him and managed to stay focused.

Later:

Well, I did my time today. Completed 13 cases which is considerably less than 25. Hopefully, I'll complete the others tomorrow. Administrators met again all day today. They're supposed to be working out who goes where for training. They actually started meeting last Thursday. I've never seen anything like it.

We're finally rolling. This doggone #82 takes forever to take off. We've been sitting here for about fifteen minutes. Believe me when I tell you, those minutes tick away as slowly as melting ice!

This poem flashed in my mind last night as if it was being dictated to me, I got it all down in a few minutes, inspired from that church sermon on Saturday:

The congregation stood enraptured, all praises to the Holy Son. The sermon had been a very meaningful one.
In the front row stood a sister whose child had been missing. Loudly she wailed, her face glistening
Reverend spoke of it during the sermon, how the child was returned early that morning
'A child's come home'
It was moving and others began crying as well. Thoughts of their own children and how it must have been hell.
Raised 'by the village' this child had been. Fed and chastised by neighbors and kin

Taken by a young brother to make his mark. To prove to the gang he
  was a man and had heart

The child was to be sold to a faction upstate. To work the streets of New
  York, to whore and be raped

But a member of the gang felt a pang and rebelled. Awoke in the night,
  released her from her cell

Full of remorse alone and undercover, he wrapped her in his black coat
  and returned her to her mother

A woman asked the mother how did you sleep? not knowing if your
  child lived or had food to eat

The woman replied I do have a story, full of love hate anguish and glory

But to you my dear sister all I will say, is I looked to the clouds and saw
  they were grey

But someone once told me long ago, to seek the Creator and just let it
  flow

So I stretched forth my hand in spite of my sight, and parted the gray
  clouds and behold there was light

'A child's come home'

As I said, it was a stirring sermon indeed.

7/8/98
Journal Entry

Productive day. Got a lot done. Found out where the SUCCESS training will be held. Three days in Savannah for Employment Services training. Ten days for TANF and Food Stamp training will be held at the CNN office downtown. Supposedly, we'll be provided imbursement up front for our rooms and food for Savannah. This is good. I can deal with that. And what's not to love about Savannah!

I just stopped at my little store in Five Points where I normally buy cigarettes and picked up soda, tomato sauce and cigarettes. It was either that or stop at Kroger's, too hot for that. I'm exhausted. A few more stops and I'm home. My stomach is a mess. Ate too late last night. My favorite hot wings. Later. Peace

7/9/98
Journal Entry

I stayed up until 4:00 am, talking with Paul. We discussed some of everything. From ten years ago and a good friend of his (a friend who helped him get into his first recovery program) Ella Ferndale, to Clayton Sr.'s death to Tonya and Omar's marriage this year. We covered a lot of ground. This culminated in Paul placing a phone call to Ella. They reminisced for a time, both glad to hear from each other. I didn't mind at all, I met her back when she tried to help Paul and she went out of her way to assure me that she wasn't interested in a relationship with him. In fact she was a social worker at a homeless shelter. Back then she'd given Paul a copy of 'A Course in Miracles' which, over time, became my 'rock.'

I'm on Intake this morning. Hope it's not too busy, I need to complete Food Stamp reviews and re-open cases.

Father, please help me to help myself. The conflict I'm feeling is taking a toll on me. The peace and trust that I seek continues to elude me. I need it now. I seek it now. I have it now. Thank you. Thank you. Thank you.

The Black Cultural Weekend began already. I hope to make a couple of events tomorrow. We'll see.

7/13/98
Journal Entry

Trying day. Paul called me from Grady Memorial Hospital. Bless him or damn him, I don't know, but I'm so thankful that he's safe!

I called his shrink at VA, Dr. Saldina. I explained that he's been hospitalized in bad condition. She said for him to get to the VA hospital first thing in the morning. She also says he must participate in their program at VA in order for them to treat his depression. That's the bottom line. He's got to cooperate with them to receive their help. She also knows he's dirty.

I'm going straight to the crib (I used to love that word!). All I had was about two hours sleep this morning, so I know I'm going to crash early. This stress!

7/14/98
Journal Entry

P aul came home last night after he was released from Grady. He got up and went to the VA this morning. He wasn't processed in until after noon. He called me at 1:00 o'clock.

"Dr. Saldina read me the riot act," he said.

"I knew she would, Paul."

"She wants me to go to a half-way house and shit," he said.

"Do what she says, Paul. Sixty days, ninety days, whatever. You've got to cooperate with those people in order to support your disability claim as well as for your sobriety.

"Man, do you know how long I'd last in one of those places? People telling you what to do and how to do it all day long?"

"You can do it for a little while," I said.

"I'd last about thirty minutes if that long, man. Anyway, I've got to go. This nurse was gracious enough to give me some change and I tried to call you earlier but you weren't at your desk, apparently. She's standing here looking in my mouth (he chuckled for her benefit), so I'll talk to you later, okay?"

"Alright, I'll call you later this evening after I get home," I said.

7/15/98
Journal Entry

I called Paul last night when I got home, which was after 7:30. I'd gotten this bright idea that I'd go to this particular furniture store in Forest Park to check it out. The bus didn't go that far up Jonesboro Road because it turns into Clayton County and all that kind of nonsense. Who knew this shit! To make a long story short, I caught the bus back to East Point without accomplishing anything. Just your typical day in Atlanta on public transportation, thank you.

Paul was in pretty good spirits when I called. He said he was playing spades.

"You don't even want to play scrabble or anything when you're at home anymore," I said.

"Hey, when you're in a place like this, about the only thing you can do is shit like this to keep your sanity."

We talked about him entering a half-way house again.

"It's easy for you to tell me how easy it would be for me to go there, you don't have to do it. Let's not even discuss it anymore because the fact of the matter is, no matter what you say to me, if I don't want to go, I'm not going. So let's not do this, okay, June?" I said nothing.

7/18/98
Journal Entry

I'm out here rolling on the East-bound train to Decatur, going to see Paul at the VA hospital. Man it is hot! I took a long relaxing bath instead of showering before leaving the house, but already, I feel like an oily dish rag!

John's CD is awesome. He's one talented brother (and a colleague). I taped his hit song on my little tape to take to the hospital for Paul. It certainly lifted my spirits.

My days are full. Today I've got to get back on the southwest side and pick up a few things at the drugstore. I'm seriously thinking about getting some Rum for Daiquiri's and a couple of movies. After-all, I've got to run the sweeper, and make a decent home-cooked meal, which my body is craving. Shopping will be limited to paper products, etc.

We're grooving (yeah right) at the Decatur station, but as I speak, we take off. That's one thing about this #19 VA bus, it doesn't sit forever. I should reach the hospital no later than 12:30 if the woman on the north-bound train gave me the correct information a while ago.

I called my sister last night. We discussed mom's house. She's putting it up for sale, mom's in a long-term care facility. I told her I'd consider buying it.

I'm on the #82 getting ready to make my last stop and head on in. Paul appreciated the things I bought him. I must say it was worth it to see him smile. He didn't have much to say about the tape. He spoke briefly about the half-way house. Says he agreed to cooperate with Dr.

Saldina. He says VA will only pay for thirty days and that that's the longest he'll stay.

"They want six hundred dollars or more a month to stay in those places," he said.

"That much?"

"Yeah, and you know I'm not about to pay them out of my pocket."

Frankly, I'm amazed that he's agreed to go for any length of time. God is good. Then too, Dr. Saldina don't play. So we'll see.

I joined Paul and played Bid Whist with a couple of male patients. It was a decent game. We set them three times and won. By then it was close to 4:00 o'clock and dinner was about to be served. It was time for me to leave.

We're finally rolling. It is incredibly hot! The humidity makes it almost unbearable for me. I tell you, once I get in, there's no plans to go back out until Monday morning!

I'm going to have to pass on the Black Cultural activities at Greenbriar Mall. Man I hate that. There is always great art, artist and books and beautiful African garb to get lost in! I just can't make it. It's all about the heat!

8/13/98

"The balustrade rose slowly and stealthily upward like a long black Cobra." Those are the words I was speaking as I awoke from a crazy dream this morning. I can't remember anything else but my body was tense and I was breathing really heavy as if I'd been running.

It's been a minute, G. All thanks to the Creator for waking me this morning. For my health, strength and courage. There is much to be thankful for, I can't begin to list them all here. However, I must express gratitude for all things. In the name of Jesus Christ and all of the Holy ones before and after Him. Amen.

Candice, behind me in training, just gave me her office number. She wants information on where we're going to be staying in Savannah. I left my paperwork at the office. She's hilarious, kept me laughing during the session. Hope I didn't miss anything important, clowning around with her.

Thanks for getting me through this tedious training. Amen.

8/14/98
Journal Entry

T his is payday for me. Paul didn't try to hit me up for any money, however, he was honest enough to admit today is going to be a real trial for him. At first he said he's going to an NA meeting on Simpson road, which means he'll have to go through the 'trap' areas to get there. I didn't feel too good about that and suggested he stay in out of the rain and just attend his evening meeting at 8:00 tonight. He said he wanted to make both meetings and decided to call Malcolm and see if he'd be willing to come by and take him to this particular meeting. I thought that might work, but I said nothing.

9/3/98
Journal Entry

C ongratulations, Paul! You're approaching sixty days clean. It was wonderful to see you smiling, upbeat and in good spirits this morning. I've waited a long time for this day! God truly is good.

I'm also feeling confident that we will have more good news about Ransom this evening. At this point all I can do is give thanks. I've been moaning and praying sorrowfully for so long. Thank you, Father. Today, I pray for all the people of the world, that they may bring all of their burdens to you and leave them there. I pray that we will all become consciously thankful.

It's cloudy and windy this morning. The clouds are a dingy-gray. My plan is to get down the hill before there is a down-pour. I left the extra umbrella for Paul this morning since I left mine somewhere on Tuesday, don't know where. But this is his day. I want him to enjoy it without being concerned about getting caught in the rain. Guess I'm more concerned about him than I am myself this morning, but it's all good. He was hilarious before I left the house, going on and on about how he'd impress his group today with his new wardrobe and fresh hair-cut.

9/10/98
Journal Entry

Paul's been working his NA program for about two months now. Bought new clothes, shoes and takes showers daily again! Amen, somebody!

Ransom was released from London Correctional Institute last week. He's now at Franklin County Jail in Columbus, Ohio. He'll be there until Oct 1st when the judge decides which half-way house or other facility he wants him to reside in. Things have been happening so fast, I haven't had time to adjust to them. Can't express how thankful I am, however.

Paul attends two and three meetings a day. It's almost like he's going to work every day, except for the fact that there is no additional money coming in. But in a sense it is because he's allowing me to keep his VA funds and issue him money to cover his transportation and other daily expenses AND he's not getting money from me! Can you believe it, G?

As for me, I've been feeling very sleepy lately. Falling asleep on the train, at my desk and everything. Just not getting enough rest, I guess. For one thing, Paul's new-found sobriety has him bright-eyed early each morning. He's been waking me at ungodly hours, giddy with plans for the future and wanting to talk! Well, you know me, G, I can't get back to sleep once I'm fully awake. I still suffer from insomnia and I'm lucky to get to sleep in the first place. Then again, maybe all the sleepless nights spent worrying and obsessing have finally caught up with me. I don't know.

The sun is shining directly in my face as I'm out here rolling on the south-bound to Garnett Station.

9/12/98
Journal Entry

I'm out here rolling on the North-bound train to Five Points and from there I'll take the East-bound to Eastlake Station.

Yesterday, I went to Kaiser and got my Mammogram completed. From there I phoned in for an appointment at the Cascade Facility. My primary care doctor, Dr. Meadows, listened to my complaints and prescribed medication that he says will knock out the infection. I have a severe sinus infection which has really been kicking my ass, which explains why I've been so drained and sleepy, I suppose. Good thing I finally got myself to the doctor. He wrote prescriptions for penicillin, two sinus medications to be taken together and a nasal spray. Actually, I can feel this stuff working already, but I still feel drained.

Paul and I got up at five this morning and went grocery shopping at Kroger's. It felt good to get the shopping done and the kitchen cleaned before eight. Afterwards, we had a light breakfast, I took my meds and got myself together to meet with the writers.

We met at the Callibo Coffee Shop in Decatur. It's a quaint little artsy place with large photos of writers on the walls and soft jazz oozing in the background. Nice atmosphere. The meeting went well. Paula volunteered to contact Marta regarding the billboard. A couple of the writers would like to get some of their poems on the billboards on the trains. The young dread-locked filmmaker who was a guest at our last meeting in Colony Square surprised us by showing up again as he said he would. We began a discussion about relationships and the Women's movement. This brother gave a passionate portrayal of the dating scene out there. He said and I quote, "Women used to want equal pay and good jobs and to be treated fairly. Now they want penises and to be with other women. They want to marry late, while the men want to marry earlier. If any problems arise, their first thought is that 'this isn't working, see ya' and they're out of there." Of course this started a rather lively round-table discussion.

Shane, the young white brother in the group, brought his mother with him, again. She appears quite young. He left a little early to show her around Atlanta.

9/14/98
Journal Entry

T hanks to the Creator for waking me this morning. Thanks too, for the blessings of all man-kind.

I hope that President Clinton will not be impeached or forced to resign. Whatever. Politics!

It's Monday morning and the #83 is rolling into Oakland City Station. I think the meds for my sinusitis has really taken effect. And, check this out, I also requested a referral for mental health counseling when I went in on Friday. Dr. Meadows seemed reluctant, but he gave me one. Which reminds me, I need to call for an appointment today or tomorrow.

Paul is still handling his business. He's continuing with the daily meetings. All praises to The Most High!

It's very humid this morning, expecting 90 degrees today, which is crazy in Atlanta when you factor in the humidity.

Just arrived at Oakland City. Obviously, we just missed a train.

I'm feeling proud. Fixed my lunch last night and don't have to spend money today. Also, my energy level is returning. Sometimes it's the little things.

9/15/98
Journal Entry

This morning began well. Paul insisted that I sit down and balance my check book which I did without resistance. It feels good not to be stressed out on pay day, even if the money is a little tight. There's a small sense of freedom. The bills are current and I'm handling my personal stuff, getting a better handle on what I'm spending.

Paul looks good and says he feels good. He's wearing clean fresh clothing and his hair is nicely cut, almost like his old self. He's talking about how he's sharing his blessings in the meetings and he's looking forward to attending noon-day meetings daily. It's all good.

I phoned Kaiser's appointment line and made an appointment for Behavioral Health counseling. For some reason I assumed it would be scheduled weeks from now, however, they wanted to schedule me for this week. I'm not ready for that! I don't really feel ready for next week but I agreed to go. I need it.

I'm going to Bible-Study with Malcolm and his wife, Shirley. Paul said he may as well go to his evening meeting. Well, of course.

I'm at Oakland City and here's the train at last. Can't find a seat, I'll stand near the exit. I don't mind. People stare at me as I write standing up, I don't mind that either. Folks are sleeping, most are reading the Atlanta Journal and Constitution about Clinton, I'm sure. Others are reading novels, the Creative Loafing and other local mags. Speaking of Clinton, can you believe that they're considering Impeachment proceedings? Yes! I mean it's just amazing!

We're nearing Garnett Station. Later

9/17/98
Journal Entry

Good morning, G

I feel good this morning. I jumped out of bed shortly after the alarm went off. That's a huge step for me, the way I've been feeling lately with this sinus situation. Apparently, the worse is really over, I'm stronger. Thanks for the blessings, Father, and while I'm at it, thanks for the blessings of all mankind. Right now, I'm appreciating each exquisite moment. Thank You.

Paul and I exercised together this morning. Then we showered and read from Ianya VanZant's (lovely and inspiring sister) daily meditations. As I dressed for work, Paul prepared breakfast. Turkey bacon and egg salad on wheat toast. So I brought it along to eat at my desk this morning.

Today is the last day that we can key on PARIS at work. Our new system (SUCCESS) will go on-line Saturday. So Monday the fun and games begin. It should be interesting to say the least.

9/21/98
Journal Entry

Morning, G

All Praises to the Most High. Thank you for the many blessings and well-being of my children and loved ones and for the blessings of the world.

The Clinton Video Tape in which he allegedly committed perjury will be released to the general public today via TV, the Internet and in book form. It truly is sad the way things are. I imagine we're supposed to see Clinton's disapproval rate soar after the country's had a chance to digest this. We'll see something by this evening.

Yesterday, Paul and I were pleasantly surprised when his friend and brother in recovery, Hakeem, invited us to his home for dinner. I was tired, but I'm glad we went, I enjoyed myself and I think Paul did as well. Hakeem and his wife, Carol, had planned the day well. Hakeem had Paul help him with yard work while Carol and I got to know each other. She's a gracious hostess and a great cook. After our delicious meal, we shared some hilarious moments.

Later:

On the news on WCLK, I heard that Flo Jo died. They said she died in her sleep of a heart attack. She had a history of heart trouble and my co-worker informed me that she also had Asthma. God bless her! Such a beautiful and talented athlete. What a blow to her loved ones and everyone! Sad day.

I finally buckled down and completed some work this afternoon. Got some cases ready to transfer, deleted Future-Action messages.

It rained lightly this morning, and it cooled down a bit but it may become muggy again, knowing Atlanta.

Oh yeah, I meant to talk more about our visit at Hakeem's. Carol wanted me to stay longer while Hakeem and Paul went to their NA meeting but I had already committed to go to the NA meeting with him and I really wanted to go. Carol was so relieved to share her story with me because she kept Hakeem's addiction a secret from her family and friends. She was eager for us to get together again and we exchanged numbers.

The meeting was very interesting, this was my first. The thing that struck me was how well each member articulated, male and female. Don't get me wrong, I'm well aware that many well-educated and intelligent people are addicted to drugs, but what I found striking is that each and every addict seems well able to express him or herself regardless of their background.

I stayed up watching Showtime movies last night. There were two good ones. 'The Game' with Michael Douglas, which I'd already seen but I still enjoyed it. And 'Gridlocked' with Tupac Shakur, which was much better than I expected. I slept for about an hour this morning! Needless to say, I was quite sleepy at work today. Still am.

9/29/98
Journal Entry

Evening:

I t's 6:00 pm and I just left work, which is unusual for me since we went off of Flex-time and get off at 4:30. But I had to pull fifty cases for Barbara Weaver (we all had to do it) of clients who aren't participating in any type of work activity. I've got quite a few of them and it is really time-consuming pulling them. I pulled forty-eight. Tomorrow, I'll pull two more.

There's one of Atlanta's Finest on the train, near the entrance. His hand is resting on his gun. Looks no more than 18 years old.

Paul should be gone when I get home. When I spoke to him earlier, he said he was leaving for a meeting at 6:30.

Still raining out, hope it continues through the night, good sleeping weather.

10/3/98
Journal Entry

P aul and I got up this morning and went to Kroger and bought stuff on sale. He gave me two hundred dollars and then returned his bank card to me. The brother is truly making strides with his sobriety. This addiction thing is no joke!!

I am at peace in the Lord. I fear no man nor situation. The Power of the Creator resides in me! This will

be a productive day.

10/6/98
Journal Entry

Morning, G

It's a wonderful morning. Thanks to the Glorious Creator for the blessings of the world.

Paul is gregarious as ever! He's up early daily writing letters, praying and meditating. It's something to witness. He's exercising with me. God is good. His VA claim for increased benefits was recently denied (he's still fighting to get 100%) and he didn't go off the deep end. He simply waxed philosophical about it and proceeded to file a rebuttal. "What's for me is for me," he said. What! Also, he's decided to obtain legal counsel. I've kept myself out of the way. I'm learning how to do that, G.

10/8/98
Journal Entry

Today, I'm sending a letter to payroll to cease taking money out of my salary for legal insurance, what a rip-off, worthless! Also, Paul wrote a letter to our Apartment Complex and I made a copy. This is a progression of the previous letters which we don't believe they received from management requesting a rental reduction due to hot water issues. Who knows whether we'll get it or not. They may even attempt to terminate the lease, either now or when the lease is up. Whatever. One really must stand for something.

10/9/98

TGIF! I plan to be productive as well as have some fun.

Dammit, missed that North-bound train by just a few seconds! The doors were closing and I heard the bell chime as I bounded up the escalator.

Now we're rolling north. I really do enjoy the train, but you can't really appreciate it's beauty and efficiency when you're traveling to work. It's much more of an interesting activity when traveling leisurely, which I do on weekends. The scenic view is quite nice when you take the time to notice it. When I first moved to Atlanta and rode it for the first time, I felt like a kid watching the throngs of people boarding and un-boarding and all the colorful sites at each stop.

This morning, Paul apologized for going off yesterday. It was really nonsense. He had lectured me about looking at all the sales in the paper. "Winn Dixie is having a sale on orange juice, buy one/ get one free. We should jump on this, you don't seem to care, how do you ever expect to save and get ahead?" It wasn't so much what he was saying, but the way he said it. Pissed me the hell off, I'm sitting there across from him at the table thinking, "Bro, all the money you've blown out there in the streets on drugs—thousands of dollars, and you're going to preach to me about saving a couple of dollars! I didn't actually say this, I was already over it (I'm growing, choose your battles!) because I'm aware that structure and making daily choices is important to his recovery so I said a silent 'kiss my ass' in my mind and kept it moving. It's refreshing to get an apology, however, tells me he's taking personal inventory and trying to come correct. I accepted it, graciously.

10/19/98
Journal Entry

The Writer's Group meeting was interesting as expected, we all seemed to vibe positively. Also, the Support Group meeting that two mutual friends and I formed shows promise. Carol (Hakeem's wife) and Shirley (Malcolm's wife) and I decided to form our own Support Group. I'd suggested that the two of them attend the Al-anon group that I sometimes attend instead of re-inventing the wheel, but neither of them were on board. Carol is still wrestling with sharing Hakeem's addiction with her family, even though his employer has placed him into rehab several times in the past (he's a top-paid computer person at a large company) apparently, they don't want to let him go. Shirley is deeply religious and involved with her church. Malcolm got clean after she got him to join and today he is a deacon and devotes much of his time working with addicts in the church as well as the ones in the streets. He doesn't follow any twelve-step program but says he has nothing against it.

12/16/98
Journal Entry

Morning, G,
Thanks for the knowledge of your presence, some days you seem closer than ever, you're like a light breeze on my left cheek, it's amazing. No one would believe me, but I know you're real, I know you've got my back. It's been a while since I've checked in, things have been going okay, however, it's been crazier than ever at the office with Christmas upon us.

Paul got himself a coat for Christmas. Well, not really for Christmas, he needed one badly. I got myself a simple little long black dress and two pairs of earrings. They have some great prices at Burlington's. I'm going to check them out more often. The air is crispy and cool this morning, it's in the low sixty's. Nice.

Later:

Today was something. Actually it was crazy!

First off, Amanda Whitehouse, a General Assistance case manager, greets me at the elevator before I even reached my office.

"Jack Miles is downstairs to see ya, she said.

"Who is Jack Miles?" I asked. I had to hide my annoyance, Whitehouse's wide toothy grin irritated me this early in the morning, she always appears unreasonably pleasant. However, she's good people, like a breath of fresh air, really. Most of my colleagues, including me, hover between total burn-out and Prosac. All day long we greet each other with a silent shaking of the head which translated means poor me, this job is a trip, ain't it, girlfriend? Lord have mercy, I'm so stressed!' Over time and for my own well-being, I've re-interpreted this head shake to mean; I've got an interesting career helping people, one which gives me more satisfaction than most of the sisters in my circle get from their significantly higher salaries in private industry. On a good day I make a difference in people's lives. It's just that there's not enough time in the day. I love what I do, otherwise, I would've left this madness long ago. "Mr. Miles is the client I just transferred to you. He gets Supplemental Security Income and he's an alcoholic. Harmless, really, but he can be a pain. Want me to see him for you?" Her grin was so wide, I thought her face would split open!

"It's fine, I'll see him." I left her at the elevator. All that brightness in her face made my eyes hurt. It was too early in the morning.

The smell of cheap liquor hit me as soon as Mr. Miles sat down at my desk. He was a lean, healthy looking guy who appeared to be in his early sixties and in spite of his drinking, he was still handsome and well-groomed. His gray pants and white sports shirt were neatly pressed and his salt and pepper hair was partly crowned with a multi-colored Kufi hat.

"I apologize for the delay, Mr. Miles, I'm Ms. Calloway," I said. " How may I help you today?"

"Sixty dollars in Food Stamps just ain't enough," he said. His voice was deep and raspy kind of like Ray Charles. I turned slightly, away from the alcohol fumes. It was too early in the morning.

"You need to review my case and do something about that, Ms. Calloway." He emphasized the C when he said my name. I nodded and maintained eye-contact. His eyes held no anger, it was only in his voice when he spoke.

"And I need tokens to get to some kind of shelter. It's raining out there and I ain't got no money."

"I'll see what I can do," I said. He went on as if I hadn't spoken.

"Ms. Whitehouse took care me. She's a beautiful lady. She's real people." He began to sing; "I---am everyday peo-ple." He drummed his hands on the desk. "I----am everyday peo-ple. Yeah man. Ms.

Whitehouse, she take care business. I bet you ain't about nothing. Bet you gonna give me a hard time."

It took nearly two hours with Mr. Miles and after I certified him for Food Stamps, provided him with tokens to catch the train and called around to several shelters on his behalf, he had the nerve to call me a bitch! Not to my face, but when he thought I wasn't within earshot. I was returning with his tokens when I over-heard him.

"Bitch got me waitin' round all day, givin' me the fuckin run-around."

Ms. Soperton, my next client, didn't have an appointment but insisted on being seen.

"I see that you had an appointment two weeks ago, Ms. Soperton," I said.

"Yeah, well, I was sick and couldn't make it. That's why I came today. I need my Food Stamps" Ms. Soperton is small and shapely with thin brown card-board color dread-locks. She is clearly white but she speaks the language of the 'hood.' I thumbed quickly through her case file and then accessed the computer.

"I see that you have moved, do you have a current lease or rent receipt," I asked.

"Naw, but ah you can call CJ. He's the one I rent a room from." I see on the system that she's receiving benefits which aren't included in her FS budget.

"How long have you been receiving SSI, Ms. Soperton?" She rolls her eyes at me.

"What you mean?" she said loudly. "I thought they notified yall about that, I don't feel like going through no changes, man. You know?" She reared back into her chair and did the neck and head-twisting thing, her hands balled into fist to show me she meant business.

"I understand, Ms. Soperton." I deliberately lowered my voice, hoping she would do the same. "But you will have to verify your residence and we will have to include the SSI benefits in your budget. Naturally, you'll get fewer Stamps."

"Look, I ain't got time for this. You askin' me all these questions and talkin' about cutting my Food Stamps!"

"Just calm down," I said.

"Like I said, I ain't got time. You can close my fuckin case, just close my fuckin case. I'm sick as a dog, ain't got time."

Suddenly, I was very tired. I tried again. "Maybe you'd like to come back on another day when you're feeling better and we can see what we can do.

"You can just close my fuckin case, man. Bitches act like the money's comin' out of your pockets!" She jumped up and ran out of my office. I sat there playing with my "Covey's Seven Habits of Successful People' pen. It was a forest green, my favorite color. Two bitches in one day. Boy was I on a roll. Usually, I only got that distinction once or twice a year!

The old woman who'd been sitting in the back of the waiting room was my last client of the day, an Intake application. She did not answer when I called her name, a strange name... Crystal Christmas. After calling her name again and checking the first-floor bathroom, I gave up and gratefully returned to my office. The last thing I needed was another long-winded, needy client this time of the day, anyway. Most days, my clients are positive, agreeable, trying-to-get themselves-together type people. Just occasional rough-necks, but it never fails that the approach of Christmas brings out the depressed sad ones with the most dreadful stories. This has been going on all week. Just as in the general population, I suppose. Doesn't just about everyone expect some kind of magic at Christmas? And aren't they always disappointed? As if someone or something has failed to come through for them. This goes on year after year, and sometimes I get caught up in it as well.

I stopped in my tracks at my office door. The old woman was sitting quietly at my desk. She was strange-looking for sure. Raisin-wrinkled face, I mean her entire face was wrinkled. Unusual for a black woman, I thought. She turned and looked at me and I saw that her eyes were deep and smoky, there was only a dot of white at the edges of each of her eyes, it was startling. Her hair was huge and natural with streaks of black, gray, red and blue. This would not have been a big deal on one of my younger clients, I see it all the time. But this woman appeared ancient and out of place.

"Are you Mrs. Christmas?" I asked.

"Yes, it's Crystal Christmas, sweetie." She had a sneer or smile on her face, I couldn't tell which. I eyed her hesitantly, I mean, her name and the way she appeared in my office.

"Mrs., ah, Christmas, do you have a driver's license or a state ID?"

"Yes, sweetie." She whipped out her ID. A whiff of moth-ball smell drifted from her purse. Odd too.

"I'll have to make a copy." Indeed her name was Crystal Christmas." You're applying for food stamps, right?"

"Yes, sweetie." Her manner was kindly enough but that 'sweetie' thing was getting old fast. I resisted the urge to tell her that a simple yes or no would do.

With a few more questions I got her certified and ushered her out of my office. Another odd thing, no one saw her leave, not the two other co-workers in the building nor the security guard who remained at the entrance to let clients in and out after-hours. He swore he didn't let her out, in fact he says he never let her in, that he never saw her! I need your help with this one, G!

Later:

Made it through the day, what a day! Right now the Atlanta skyline is beautiful. It's dark already. The edge of the sky is orange with a little pink in some areas. There's water on the factory rooftops. In the dimness, it gleams like snow.

I called Paul from Five Points to let him know that I have to stop and pay the electric bill and pick up some Christmas cards. I may get a couple of Christmas Stockings to hang on the stairway. That would be cute.

We're here at Oakland City Station. Later.

12/17/98
Journal Entry

I feel wonderful this morning, G! All thanks to the Creator.

Meditation:

All thanks to the Most High for our many blessings. Thank you for your Magnificent Guidance, Assurance, Love, Truth and Beauty. Thank you for your Knowledge, Grace and Help, without which we could not even rise in the morning. All my love flows back to You Who first extended it. Who first released it. Who first gave it. Bless all of our parts who are in suffering and misery. Last but not least, thanks in advance for blessing this day and all that it contains as we as colleagues come together in peace and understanding. In the name of Jesus and in the name of all Saints, I pray. Amen.

Ransom called night before last, Keith called last night. They are both something else, these sons of mine. I am blessed with these two wonderful guys.

12/18/98

Evening:

Today was productive and peaceful. Mandy bought Christmas gifts for the entire unit. We were expecting cash because that's what she usually gives. I got a nice make-up bag. We all ate too much. Angela brought Nachos and a beef and cheese dip that she made which was very good. She also made chocolate chip cookies which were tasty as well. I'm not hungry now but I'll probably make wings tonight. Love those things! As hot as I can stand them! And I've fallen in love with Ranch dressing.

I'm going straight home this evening. For one thing, I'm exhausted, for another, it's already dark and I'd like to get there before Paul leaves for his NA meeting. I'll finish shopping tomorrow.

12/21/98
Journal Entry

G ood Morning, G
 What a great morning to be alive! Thanks to the Most High for
all blessings. Amen

It's Monday. Only two more working days before my Christmas
begins. I must tell you that I am ecstatic. I get to spend my days as I
please for the next eleven days!

06/26/00
Journal Entry

Man, it's been a long time since I've checked in! Things have been mostly good and also, I've been driving, yeah, got a car but it's on the blink and we've decided not to put any more money into it. Saving for a new one.

I've missed riding the train. I've said it before, it's so lively, so many wonderful faces and colors, and beautiful clothing, especially that worn by the women. And the smells, wonderful mingling of cologne and after-shave. Mingling conversations. Snatches of interesting dialogue here, gossip over there, business discussions over there. Weird stares. Weather is pleasant this morning, not too humid, but it promises to be another scorcher later.

There's a brother that just boarded the train. He approached a high-yellow sister. "I like light-skinned women better than dark women," he said loudly. The sister tried to ignore him (as did most of us sisters who were sitting and standing near them, and we covered the spectrum from deepest mahogany to lightest beige). She looked rather perplexed. I know she couldn't believe this fool actually said what he said. He rambled on, in a high-pitch tone, obviously wanting attention. He was a cinnamon-brown, not light at all. I hate to admit it, but his words really pissed me off. A part of me wanted him to say something to me. I wanted to tell him how truly ignorant he was---that he had a slave-mentality. I wanted to ask him why he felt the need to say such a thing in the midst of all the white folks, who by the way were pretending to ignore him. Ah well, such is life. You can't let all the ignorance get to you, and folks have a right to their own opinions and taste, no matter how uninformed and shallow they may be. But it's sad that in the year 2000, a new millennium, black folks not only harbor this archaic thinking but that they have the audacity to speak it. Peace, I'll let it go.

Paul and I were at it yesterday, not really arguing but mainly venting and letting each other know how we feel. It wasn't about much, really, but this is new for us. Personally, I think it's much healthier than the silence of the past; him lying on the chair not saying anything and me going about the day as if everything's fine, yet angry and stressed out. So I welcomed it. Cleared the air. It's a new day.

We're at Oakland city, here comes the train. I'm on Intake today, I'll make the most of it. I've also got to get my monthly report done and turn it in on time. We're off Monday and Tuesday for the Fourth of July. I'm thinking about putting something on the grill, a couple slabs of ribs, maybe a couple of Ribeye's.

Wow, we've celebrated Christmas twice since the last time I passed this way. Well, I must tell you that there were no calamities, no drama or anything to write home about and in our life, that's a good thing. Life is good.

09/18/00
Journal Entry

Good Morning, G

Been a while, hasn't it. Life's just been happening, mostly good. As of last week, Paul began an intensive program with the VA. He's required to attend every day for thirty days. He's studying the work-book which is pretty deep stuff. This weekend he went to a noon-day meeting on Saturday and yesterday he went to church with Hakeem. They went to the Shrine of the Black Madonna. Hakeem is a member there. After church, they went to a meeting at Barbara King's church, held in the Day Care Center. I was glad to see that. I love her church and attend there occasionally. I'm not aware of any other black churches in the neighborhood that hold NA or AA meetings at their facilities which I find amazing given that our communities are the hardest hit with the Crack epidemic! Paul is impressed also. He's agreed to attend her church with me based on that. We'll see. This morning he was up at five o'clock, all lively and feeling good working in his work-book.

As for me, I'm keeping it real, allowing him to do his thing. It's in the Creator's Hands.

This train is crowded this morning, folks standing and breathing all over each other. This brother next to me appears out of it, head down, asleep. Smelly, soiled clothing, possibly homeless. Bless you, my brother!

I'm on Intake this morning, not thrilled with that on a Monday morning. So be it.

10/19/00
Journal Entry

Out here rolling on the Southbound to Oakland City station. Going to an Al-Anon meeting, just left work. This meeting is being held at Bernice King's Church on Stanton Road. Yeah, another black church in the community. Interestingly enough, this is one of the churches I joined years ago when I was seeking a church home. Back then, I would attend a church two or three times, join it, and then stop going. Don't ask me why, I don't know. Ms. King wasn't the minister there then, however. I doubt if she's involved with this group, but then again, you never know. She's such a dynamic sister----connected with the pulse of the community. Just for the record, Bernice King is the daughter of the Rev. Martin Luther King Jr.

Paul didn't answer when I called home, he'd left a message earlier, letting me know that he was home. Obviously, he went to Noon-day today. I'm not worried, this thing is God-run, right, G. All we have to do is keep ourselves out of the way.

Ransom called yesterday. Says he's doing well. He goes to the Salvation Army on Monday. He has to stay there for six months. He's come a long way. God is good.

3/19/01
Journal Entry

H i, G
Been a while, hasn't it. I'm grateful for many things today. Ransom graduates from his program next month, I believe it's April 25th. Paul's doing well, attending NA and AA meetings three days weekly. He's got his head on straight. Just for today, as they say. We're working an austerity program, our immediate goal is to get another car. Long term, to purchase a home.

Out here rolling on the #82 headed toward Camp Creek Market Place. Man, was I sick yesterday---after a culmination of days in which I could feel it coming on, I was finally laid up. Actually, I got up, showered and started out the door when suddenly, my stomach did a flip-flop and I rushed back in and ran to the bathroom. I was bent over the sink with my hands on my head when Paul came in and looked at me.

"You can't go to work, don't make any sense. Not going to be able to do anything, why torture yourself?"

"I really need to be there," I said. There's a lot going on and I don't need to be behind and besides I'm off tomorrow."

"Fuck all that, you can only do what you can do."

"Ugh! I groaned. I wound up back in bed after making myself a bowl of grits (which was difficult to get down). I stayed there all day and only got up long enough to make some homemade soup which turned out to be really good. Gradually, my stomach started to act like it had some sense. Got a good night's sleep last night and got up on time this morning. Paul came into the bathroom and stood in front of one of the twin sinks observing me as I oiled my braids this morning preparing for work. "You look good, baby, glad you're feeling better."

Atlanta's skyline is beautiful this morning. It's supposed to reach the 70's today. Feels good right now. The sun's shining brightly, leaving a hint of gold over everything. The sky is a fairy-tale blue, like a creamy blue and white cake. Like the ocean. That's Atlanta. And that blue reminds me of Paul. Blue is his favorite color. I always took the color blue for granted. It's so naturally beautiful, it's just there. But today, when I see the color blue, I see it through Paul's eyes and it astounds me. Also, it doesn't hurt that when Paul first 'hit' on me many years ago, I was wearing Royal blue. It looked really good on me, did something for my complexion. That's what he said when he approached me. That was his line. Really.

What a journey! We've survived. Don't get it twisted, though, the struggle is real. One day at a time.

One Love. Peace.

About the Author

ESSIE SAPP- BENSON has experienced the pain and chaos of addiction in her family while juggling a stressful state job. She had to learn how to save herself. This book was an act of self-love.

Benson is a retired state worker living in Columbus, Ohio with her husband. She is the author of 'April's Sister' a short story collection.

Printed in the United States
by Baker & Taylor Publisher Services